NO PLACE LIKE ROME

JULIE MOFFETT

Recycling programs for this product may not exist in your area.

ISBN-13: 978-1-335-08014-1

No Place Like Rome

This edition published by arrangement with Harlequin Books S.A.

www.CarinaPress.com

Printed in U.S.A.

To my two precious boys, Alexander and Lucas. While I've spent considerable time and effort teaching you all about life, it's the two of you who have taught me what life is all about. Love you always, Mom.

NO PLACE LIKE ROME

Chapter One

I've loved listening to music since I was a little girl. Not because I'm musically gifted, but because notes, themes, chords and tempo all have an intrinsic mathematical logic that speaks to me. After all, music is defined by its numeric divisions, such as a beat, a measure or a bar. Musical scales are actually harmonics based on the numerical ratios present in the Fibonacci series, which are a sequence of integers beginning at zero and one and continuing with each new number being the sum of the previous two.

I know all of this because I'm a geek first-class. My name is Lexi Carmichael and I'm a mild-mannered twenty-five-year old who, thankfully for music aficionados, is not employed in any part of the music industry. By day, I work as the Director of Information Security at a hot new cyber-intelligence firm just outside of Washington, D.C. By night, I'm a gamer, book nerd and fangirl (Bond, Star Wars, Dr. Who, Lord of the Rings). I've got long brown hair, no discernible curves and zip in the social skills department. I double-majored in mathematics and computer science at Georgetown University with a specialty in cybersecurity. Ask me to talk about a rigorous axiomatic framework or computational complexity theory, and I'm all over it. Ask me to make small talk and I'll imagine myself jumping off a bridge.

Yet here I am, dressed in my fanciest dress—okay, it's my only dress—and attending an opera at the Kennedy Center in Washington, D.C., with a man whose social skills and intellect far exceed my own. Small talk is inevitable, and I have a sad feeling that my observations on the Fibonacci series in *Don Giovanni* won't fill more than a few minutes.

My acquaintance's name is Slash, which is short for "backslash" in hacker lingo. I'm pretty decent myself at the keyboard, but Slash is a hacker of extraordinary ability. Of course, Slash isn't his real name but so far he's never felt compelled to tell me what his family named him at birth. In fact everything about Slash is a mystery, except that he assures me he's Italian-American and he works, at least partially, for the NSA, where I was once gainfully employed. He's so good at what he does that he's watched around the clock by a team of FBI agents who I'm pretty sure are instructed to kill him rather than let him fall into enemy hands.

Tonight, Slash looked jaw-droppingly handsome in three-piece suit and tie. I think this isn't a date because I'm quasi-seeing my boss, Finn Shaughnessy, and Slash knows that. But Finn's and my situation is fraught with complications and I'm having a hard time sorting it all out. Maybe Slash doesn't care about Finn or maybe he does. I wouldn't know either way. Technically, the word *date* wasn't mentioned once in relation to our evening. So, as far as I know, this is just Slash's goodwill gesture to expand my personal horizons into areas, up until now, unexplored.

Slash led me to the coatroom and graciously eased me out of my coat. November could get rather chilly in Washington, D.C. and my dress was more of a light summer garment. But seeing as how it was the only suitable choice in my closet, I had to make do by wearing a pinned shawl around my shoulders and chest, partially to keep me warm and partially to hide the fact that it was scandalously low-cut in the front. I don't normally wear such revealing clothes, but my best friend Basia made me. Slash didn't have a jacket other than the one he wore with his suit, but it didn't matter. I could feel the heat radiating off him. I nearly jumped when his hot fingers brushed my bare shoulders as he removed my coat.

He took me by the elbow and steered me toward the auditorium. I was a little nervous about my first trip to the opera, but I had recently adopted a new mantra in my life—accept and embrace change. I'm not the kind of girl who likes trying new things, but after a couple of near-death experiences, I was doing my best to venture outside my safe virtual cocoon and live life to its fullest. Truthfully, I would have much rather been at home in front of my laptop engaging in an online role-playing game called GURPS and eating a big bowl of cornflakes. But I was determined to be true to my new mantra, and tonight that meant attending an Italian opera with a hacker so hot he left scorch marks on my skin.

Instead of entering the auditorium, Slash directed me down a small corridor. At the end, a security guard stood in front of an unmarked red door. Without even asking who we were, the guard quickly murmured a few words to Slash, opened the door and ushered us through.

We were backstage. A harried guy ran past me carrying a handful of costumes and another snarled at me as I accidentally stepped on a wire on the floor. Another group of people were rearranging a heavy piece of scenery while the lights dimmed and then brightened. A large red velvet curtain cast the stage in partial shadows. I barely had time to register all the activity before an enormous woman with a flowing white dress and long dark hair fashioned in sausage-like ringlets spotted us, then threw herself in our direction.

"Giovanni."

She pushed past me, nearly knocking me over, and engulfed Slash in a hug that completely hid him from sight. After a moment she began raining kisses on his cheeks and forehead, leaving a trail of red lip marks all over his face.

A guy passing by must have seen the look on my face. "Don't mind Larissa." He jerked his head. "It's all about the drama." He pulled out a clipboard, jotted something down, and moved off to the other side of the stage.

At some point, Slash finally extricated himself from Larissa's enthusiastic embrace and turned her toward me. She wore heavy white powder make-up on her face and neck, and her ample bosom mostly spilled out of a tightly cinched low-cut gown. She had a line of dark hair along her upper lip.

Slash took a handkerchief out of his breast pocket and began wiping the lipstick off his face. "Larissa, I'd like you to meet Lexi Carmichael. Larissa Dantenelli is an old friend of mine from Milan."

"Hi."

Larissa gave me a thorough and not-so-friendly perusal. "Hmmph." She let then let loose a stream of Italian. After a moment, she paused and glared at me.

Slash smiled. "Larissa says she is honored to meet you."

"Yeah, right, *Giovanni*."

His smile widened.

Turning her back on me, Larissa hooked her arm with Slash's and they spoke in low voices. Well, mostly Larissa spoke and Slash listened. After a moment, he nodded and then said to me, "She wants me to speak to her brother for a moment. I'll be right back."

With that, Slash walked away from us and disappeared behind another group of people. Larissa turned her eyes on me with laser-like intensity. I wasn't the best at reading social cues, but I didn't have to be a psychologist to see the utter dislike in her expression.

"So, your name Lexi?" she asked in heavily accented English.

I glanced in the direction Slash had disappeared, praying he'd reappear momentarily. "Yes."

"You American?"

"Yes."

"Why you here?"

Was this a trick question? "To see an opera."

"You no talk much."

"What do you want to talk about?"

Larissa gripped my arm with velociraptor-like fingernails. "I want to know how well you know my Giovanni."

I squeaked and tried to pull my arm away. "Could you clarify what you mean by 'well'?"

"Don't play dumb with me. I know what you up to."

"You do?"

She dragged me toward the red curtain with the strength of a sumo wrestler. I didn't know what she had in mind, but I tried to dig in my heels. I soon realized it was a futile effort as she outweighed me by at least one-hundred and fifty pounds.

"Giovanni never bring woman to the opera before. Not to see me. His eyes for me only."

I tried to wrench my arm from her clawed grasp. "Look, Larissa, you've got entirely the wrong idea about me."

"Do you know who I am? I world-famous soprano. People worship me. My talent is rare. It takes woman like me to be worthy of man like Giovanni. We were meant for each other. In the soul."

"Sincerely…good luck with that."

"I don't like you," Her face reddened and the tone of her voice took on a strange musical vibration.

"Jeez." I craned my neck, looking desperately for Slash Why had he left me alone with this singing psycho?

"You not woman enough for him." She gestured toward my breasts with a contemptuous harrumph. "He needs a full woman."

I'm not by nature a rude or insulting person, but I'm sensitive about the size, or non-size, of my breasts. Besides, her fingernails were making half-moons in my skin and I don't like being touched by strangers.

"Technically, Larissa, you're *full* enough for the both of us."

Larissa gasped as if I had just made the most discourteous comment in the entire free world. Maybe I had. But now I was mad and she still wouldn't let go of my freaking arm.

Her face started to turn purple beneath all the white powder and she raised her fist like she was about to punch me.

I tried to step back, but she held fast. "Whoa, lady. Really? You're going to take a swing at me?"

Her answer was to shove her meaty fist at my face. I

ducked, but she yanked hard on my arm, pulling me into her. I toppled against her with surprising force. She may have been built like a sumo wrestler, but the force of my body propelled us directly into the part of the heavy curtain. All too late, I realized what was happening.

"Crap!" I yelped with my face squashed against her bosom.

I clawed at the front of her dress with one hand, trying to get away. Unfortunately, at that exact moment, Larissa fell backward, her considerable weight taking me with her. The bodice of her gown ripped beneath my fingers with a sickening sound as the two of us fell through the opening of the curtain and hit the stage hard. We rolled across the floor like two bowling balls in a tangle of limbs. Larissa screamed as we catapulted off the stage and into the orchestra pit. For a split second my life flashed before me. People shouted, a practice scale cut off in mid-blow and then my hip and shoulder hit something hard.

For a moment I lay still, the breath knocked out of me. People were scrambling over me and a musical stand nearly brained me as it fell. When I could finally sit up, I saw two men helping Larissa to her feet. She was wailing. One boob hung out of her ripped dress and her hair was a mess. It appeared that the cellist had broken her fall. He stood, adjusting his glasses and looking a bit shaky, but it was clear he'd live. The cello, on the other hand, was a complete loss.

Someone helped me to my feet, too. I did a quick internal check, wiggling my head, hands and feet. My hip and shoulder hurt and my vision was a bit blurry, but nothing seemed injured other than my pride.

"Miss, are you okay?" someone asked and I blinked twice to get my vision back to single objects. A young man with thin hair and acne scars looked at me worriedly. "What happened?"

I ran my fingers through my hair, plucking out what was likely a piece of a violin bow. "Ahhh… I'm not sure." I looked down at the music stand I'd hit and saw the sheet music scattered across the floor. "Sorry."

"At least you missed the violin."

"There's that."

I glanced over at Larissa who was wailing, waving her arms and doing everything except gnashing her teeth. I'm sure she was enjoying all the attention. The stage manager and several technicians stood up on the stage yelling down at the people in the pit while the rest of the orchestra crew scrambled around the pit, trying to fix things. The audience was on its feet, trying to figure out what had happened.

"*Cara?*" I looked up. Slash stood on the stage, gazing down at me in surprise.

I gave him a thumbs-up and a little wave. Better to put a positive spin on things. "Hey, you."

I couldn't say anything more because I was drowned out by the stage manager, who was shouting that Larissa be taken to the hospital.

"Never." She grasped the shreds of her bodice to her breasts. "The show must go on." She marched right past the orchestra director and with a glare at me, swept up the steps and disappeared backstage. I glanced back at Slash, who frowned and crooked his finger at me.

Jeez.

I apologized once again to the acne-faced musician and met Slash at the bottom of the stage stairs.

"This way," he said, guiding me to an auditorium side door and out into the lobby. "Are you hurt?"

I adjusted my shawl, which had become tangled

around my neck, revealing a bit too much of my non-cleavage. "Mostly my pride. My hip hurts a bit."

He slid his warm hand down over my hip, rubbing his fingers in small circles on the spot. His touch was electrifying and hot. I forgot all about the hurt.

He has the ability to do that…make me forget about everything except him. We'd met last summer when we were thrown together by a set of unusual circumstances involving computers, terrorists and biotechnology. For some reason, he keeps hanging around and has a really bad habit of appearing in my life at the most inopportune moments. I don't know how to handle him or what he wants, if anything, which isn't surprising since I suck at social convention. So I'm just me and let things be what they are, which, to say the least, is baffling when it comes to Slash.

"Feel better, *cara?*"

My gaze met his and I nodded. "A little. My shoulder hurts, too."

He slid his hand beneath my shawl, lifting it a bit so he could kiss my shoulder. I tried not to jump at the incredible sensation of his lips against my skin. "You'll likely have a bruise." He adjusted the shawl and smoothed it down.

"I'm lucky I didn't break my neck."

"You've also got some scratches on your face. What happened?"

I stiffened. "In my own defense, Larissa grabbed my arm and swung at me first. I tried to get away, but she had a death grip on my arm and when she fell, there was no stopping her."

Slash raised an eyebrow.

"Okay, I may have mentioned something about her weight. But she grabbed me first, insulted my, ah, body shape and said she didn't like me. She's convinced I'm trying to steal your affections. When I tried to set her straight, she punched me. I fell into her and we rolled across the stage and into the orchestra pit."

Slash coughed. Once. Twice. Then to my surprise, he started laughing. Not a small laugh, but an honest-to-God belly laugh. I stared at him in astonishment.

"What's so funny?"

"As usual, I'm at a loss for words with you, *cara.* Truthfully, I've never known anyone brave enough to take on Larissa. But did you have to do it at the Kennedy Center in front of a full house?"

"I did *not* take her on. This was so *not* my idea. You left me alone with her." I gave him an accusing look.

"*Si*, but for less than five minutes."

"It felt like hours."

A smile twitched at his lips. "Let's go find our seats."

My mouth dropped open. "Are you serious? Go back in there after what just happened? Look at me."

I wished I hadn't said that. He gave me a slow, thorough perusal from head to toe that made me feel hot and shivery at the same time.

He touched my hair. "Do you really want to go home? I'll take you."

I didn't think it a particularly good idea to stay, but here I was, all dressed up and hanging with Slash. I really needed to expand my horizons and by God, I wasn't going to let some overwrought drama queen ruin my personal growth. Yes, my hip and shoulder throbbed, but since I wasn't going to die anytime soon, I might as well stay.

"No, I'm good."

"Are you sure?"

"I've got my game face on."

Slash smiled again and then led me to a set of stairs, which I climbed carefully in my heels. An announcement that the show would continue with just a ten-minute delay was being piped through the loudspeakers. We met a man at the top who took our tickets. He stared at me.

"Are you alright, miss? You took a hard fall."

My cheeks heated. Jeez. Apparently I'd been the main feature at the pre-show. Maybe I'd make the front page of the *Washington Post.*

"I'm fine, thanks."

Slash pressed something into his hands and he opened the door for us. We had very nice, very *private* box seats.

"Wow." I forgot all about my embarrassment. "This is ace."

Slash motioned to a seat and I sat down on a red-velvet chair. He divested himself of his suit jacket, laid it on the back of his chair then rummaged around in the pockets. To my surprise, he handed me a small pair of binoculars.

"Binoculars? What do we need these for?" I turned them over in my hand.

He sat down beside me. "You can get a closer view."

I wasn't sure I wanted a closer view, especially of Larissa, but I dutifully lifted them to my eyes and began to play with the adjustments. Not surprisingly, the binoculars were hi-tech digital. I became so fascinated with them I almost missed the opening number.

Slash lowered the binoculars from my eyes. "Relax and enjoy."

He draped his arm around the back of my chair, close, but not actually touching my shoulders. Still, I could feel the heat from his arm. It distracted me. I wasn't sure exactly what to do. Was his closeness just Slash being Slash or did it mean something else? I decided I shouldn't obsess over it and lose focus on the opera, so I folded my hands in my lap and settled in to enjoy the show.

The opera began with Larissa strolling on stage and singing. After a few minutes, I leaned over to Slash. "I don't understand a word."

"It's in Italian, *cara.*"

I knew that, but I'm pretty sure I wouldn't have understood it had it been in English either. So, what was the point? It was frustrating. I wanted to like the opera. Opera was an artistic, meaningful form of creativity. I was all for creativity. I *like* musical expression. So far, however, I wasn't getting *this* music. Maybe it was missing the rhythm or mathematical cadence I needed. Maybe I couldn't relate to it because I didn't understand the lyrics. Or maybe I was just too distracted worrying about my small boobs and wondering if Slash even noticed I had any. Not that it mattered between people who were just friends.

I glanced sideways at Slash. He didn't seem to be having a problem with the opera. Apparently, *he* got it. A true Renaissance Man. Me, on the other hand, I'm more the stereotypical geek girl.

Computers and code.

Gaming and pizza.

The girl with the really small horizon.

I tried not to sigh. The opera continued and despite the fancy costumes, incredible sets, and amazing range of the vocalists, I started to get antsy. Luckily I had the handy-dandy hi-tech binoculars on my lap. I fiddled with them and then suddenly I remembered something.

"Slash, is your real name Giovanni?"

He kept his eyes on the stage. "No."

"Larissa called you Giovanni. I heard her."

"*Cara*, my name is not Giovanni."

"Then why did she call you that?"

"It's a nickname."

"Giovanni is not a nickname. A nickname is Bill or Kate."

"Shhhh."

Larissa clutched her bosom and sang a note so high I was sure my head would explode. I wanted to stick my fingers in my ears, but I figured this would be considered anti-opera etiquette.

Leaning back in my chair, I picked up the binoculars and focused in on Larissa's upper lip. Yep, the mustache was still there.

Slash rustled beside me, pulling his cell phone out of his pocket and reading something on it. "I'm sorry, *cara*. I'm going to have to step out for a few minutes. You'll be okay?"

"Sure. As long as you don't leave me alone with any more opera singers."

He kissed me on the cheek, but a corner of his lips caught my mouth. It seemed that he lingered a bit too long and then he was gone. My heart pounded, my pulse raced.

Jeez, calm the heck down, Lexi.

It was just a friendly kiss between friends. Did friends kiss? My mother air-kissed everyone she knew. But Slash's lips had touched my mouth—no air involved. Plus, I didn't think my heart was supposed to do the tango from a "friendly" kiss.

Five minutes stretched to ten and then twenty. The opera dragged on and without Slash beside me and I totally lost track of what was going on. Not that I had a clue to begin with. It looked like I wasn't going to become much of an opera connoisseur any time soon.

I'd started tapping my feet against the box in time with the cello (the newly replaced one, I guess), wondering what the heck had happened to Slash, when the door open behind me. I turned and saw a huge bald guy dressed in tan slacks, a short-sleeved white shirt and a green tie. He came in and sat beside me. Without saying a word, he crossed his tattooed arms across his stomach and started watching the opera.

I stared at him for a moment and then cleared my throat. "Sorry, but that seat is taken."

He nodded. "Yeah. By me."

"Maybe now, but when you're not here, it's taken by someone else."

He still didn't look at me. He had a tattoo of a naked girl on his bicep. When he flexed, the naked girl jiggied her oversized breasts. I was pretty sure I couldn't move him on my own.

"Your date is busy. He got called away."

"I'm not on a date. I think. What happened?"

"Dark Stallion had an important matter to attend to. He sends his apologies."

"Dark Stallion?"

"He said to tell you he was sorry and that I should take you home after the opera is over."

"Jeez, wait. Are we talking about Slash?"

"I'm talking about your date."

"I'm not *on* a date. We're just friends."

"Whatever. He had a family emergency."

That took me by surprise. Not that Slash had a family. It's just I'd never heard him speak of his family. He'd never spoken about any friends either. In fact, I hadn't even *seen* him around anyone other than agents. He seemed the loner type, which happens to be my type, too. Maybe we were more compatible than I'd thought. Besides, I'd never told him about *my* family, so there you have it.

"Oh, well, I hope everything is okay."

I kind of wished he'd give me more information, but he stared straight ahead and focused on Larissa who was on her zillionth change of costume and was swooning and singing to some bearded guy in weird-looking pantaloons and a beret.

The opera wasn't doing it for me, so I decided to be conversational. Which meant I was really, really bored.

"You don't sing opera do you?"

He gave me a strange look. "Huh?"

"Just checking. Are you part of the FBI detail that follows Slash?"

Silence.

"Fine. Can you at least tell me your name?"

"Bald Eagle."

"That's your real name?"

"Nah, it's a nickname."

Now *that* made sense. "So, Bald Eagle, do you like the opera?"

"No. I prefer ballet."

I looked to see if he was joking, but his face remained impassive. "Slash asked you to take me home?"

"We refer to him as the Dark Stallion."

I rolled my eyes. "Fine. Did Dark Stallion ask you to take me home?"

"Yes."

"Can we go now?"

"Don't you want to see the end?"

"Truthfully I'd rather poke my eyes out with a hot stick."

He looked at me for the first time and smiled. "Thank God. I thought you'd never want to leave. Let's blow this joint."

We left the box and Baldy took me to the coat check, gave the lady a tip, then helped me into my coat.

We walked outside in the cool November air and I shivered. "So, are you friends with… Dark Stallion?"

"He doesn't have many friends."

Another thing Slash and I had in common. I could count all my friends on one hand.

"Do you know if his real name is Giovanni?"

Baldy didn't answer, only took my elbow and steered me to a black SUV that sat idling on the street. He opened the back door and I climbed in. Another large guy sat behind the wheel and gave me a little wave.

"You're done early."

"The opera didn't agree with me." As I fastened my seatbelt, an unlit red light sitting on the dashboard caught my eye. "Thanks for taking me home. I didn't know the FBI performed these kinds of services."

"We don't normally. But Dark Stallion is special."

He didn't have to say more. I already knew that, too.

They drove me home without incident. I thanked them, climbed the stairs to my apartment and went inside.

Stripping off my dress, I washed off what little makeup I had on my face, then examined the tender bruises on my shoulder and hip. They were already turning purple. I also had a scrape on my right knee and elbow. Sighing, I washed them off, then applied some antibiotic cream. Then I chased down two ibuprofen capsules with some tap water. Jeez, who knew the opera could be so dangerous?

I brushed my teeth, pulled on an oversized T-shirt

and climbed into bed. I thought I'd have trouble falling asleep, but I must have conked out immediately. At some point I began dreaming I was lost in the Italian countryside being chased by a herd of opera-singing goats. I woke up in a sweat, my heart pounding, hands shaking. Sliding out of bed, I went into the bathroom and splashed cold water on my face. After a few minutes I headed back to bed. That's when I saw the red rose on my other pillow.

Slash.

He was the only person I knew who, despite my owning a top-notch alarm system, could slip in and out of my apartment without a peep. Master hacker extraordinaire. I wondered when he had come and when he had left. Had he seen me thrashing in my sleep? Jeez, why had I put on my old, ratty T-shirt?

I picked up the rose and sniffed at it. There was a small card beneath it, so I turned it over and read the inscription.

To be continued…

I turned on the lights and looked through the rest of my apartment. Empty. The rose and the fact that my security chain had been unfastened were the only two bits of evidence that he'd been in my place. I wondered what had caused him to leave the opera so abruptly and, given the secretive nature of his work, whether he'd even be able to tell me.

Interestingly enough, I was about to find out.

It wasn't at all what I expected.

Chapter Two

I drove into the office bright and early with enough time to make a swing through Dunkin' Donuts and pick up a blueberry muffin and an extra-large coffee to go. I didn't like my fifty-minute commute from Jessup, Maryland to Crystal City, Virginia, but I hadn't yet got the courage to leave my small but cozy apartment. It was the first and only place I'd lived outside of college and I'd rented it when I started work at the NSA. Now that I worked for X-Corp Global Security and Intelligence, the commute was hell, but I was too fresh in my job to leave it just yet.

I expected to have a little free time when I got to the office. Finn, my boss and the man who I'm sort of seeing, had his family from Ireland visiting, so I figured he'd be busy with them for the next several days. We didn't have any new clients and I thought I'd surf the Net and get caught up on what was new in computer security. But when I strolled into my office, a handwritten note from Finn lay across my keyboard.

Conference Room.
#2, ASAP

I snatched my laptop in one hand and coffee in the other and headed out. When I arrived, Finn was in deep discussion with a dark-haired man whose back was to me. Still there was something familiar about that hair…

"Slash!" I dropped my laptop on the table a little harder than I expected.

Slash looked up at me and smiled. "Ah, *cara.* Good morning to you."

I waited a beat, but he made no reference to the opera. I decided to follow his example and keep my mouth shut, especially with Finn present. Not that I felt guilty or anything because, after all, it hadn't been a date. I think.

"Yeah, um, hey. I'm good. What are you doing here?"

Finn leaned back in his chair. I guess he was technically still on vacation as he was dressed in casual wear—blue jeans and a sky blue sweater, not his typical workday wardrobe.

He smiled at me. "Lexi, I'm glad you're here. Is that a scratch on your face?"

I touched my cheek. "Ah, just a little accident."

Finn exhaled a deep breath. "Well, we've got a problem."

I froze.

Oh. My. God. Slash told Finn he'd taken me to the opera and I'd made a fool of myself by falling into the orchestra pit with the lead soprano. Someone had posted pictures online—Facebook, Twitter, LinkedIn. My actions would be horrible enough to reflect badly on X-Corp and I'd have to be fired. I was *so* screwed. Sacked before I barely started.

I started to hyperventilate.

Wait. Or maybe it was something else. Something

worse. What if Finn thought Slash and I were on a date and somehow I was technically two-timing him? Like I even had a clue how to do that. Would that be considered worse than a catfight with a soprano? How would I know? Jeez. Better to fire me now and get it over with.

Finn spoke. "Slash wants to hire X-Corp."

I blinked. Slowed my breathing. Let my heart return to a semi-regular rhythm. Okay, *that* was something I hadn't expected in a million years. I felt like someone had punched me in the stomach.

"Lexi, what's wrong with you?" Finn pointed to a chair. "Sit down already. You look deathly pale and you're breathing funny."

I sat and studied Slash's face, but he looked impeccably calm. Finn jotted something down in a notebook.

"Slash's uncle has been accused of money laundering at the Vatican Bank to the tune of eighteen million euros."

"Huh?" I glanced at Slash. "Your uncle works at the Vatican Bank?"

He nodded and Finn continued. "His uncle insists it's a matter of his computer network being compromised, but the Roman authorities aren't necessarily seeing it his way."

"They think he's squirreled it away somewhere?"

Finn nodded. "Exactly. In the meantime, according to EU regulations, the Roman magistrates are freezing millions of the Vatican's money. Obviously, this is an immediate problem for the Holy Order."

I wondered if this were the family emergency that had whisked him away last night. Probably. "Okay, so where does X-Corp fit in?"

"I'd like to hire X-Corp to look into this matter on

my uncle's behalf." Slash leaned forward on the table. "He's been hacked."

I opened my laptop. "Well, it sure sounds like it. But I'd presume the Roman authorities would consider this a legit possibility and have their own experts look into it."

"True, *cara.* But their experts are not invested in my uncle's innocence and are likely not be as good as you nor as fast."

The unexpected compliment warmed me to my toes. I tried not to blush, but my cheeks heated. "Well, he has you."

There was no question that Slash was by far a more experienced and expert hacker than me, but just the fact that he thought I was decent at what I did made my heart do a little dance.

Finn ran his fingers through his hair and it looked like it wasn't the first time he'd done it this morning. "Lexi, Slash works for the U.S. government in a very sensitive position. As this is a delicate matter between the Vatican and the Roman authorities, Slash would prefer to work more behind the scenes. X-Corp would be the public face of any interaction required with the authorities."

I could deal with that. I looked over at Slash. "You think hackers compromised the Vatican? Why would they use your uncle's account?"

"He is the Director-General of the bank, the second in command. He'd have access to everything."

Wow. Who knew Slash had relatives in such distinguished places? Yet, it fit with my earlier discovery that Slash had once worked for Vatican intelligence. "Will your uncle cooperate with us?"

"Of course."

Finn made a few more notes. "When would you want us to start?"

"Today."

Finn glanced up and over at me. Something in his eyes, hesitation or uncertainty, had me pause for a moment. "Lexi. This would be your case. You're the master hacker on staff."

"Um, former hacker. Technically, I'm legit now. Mostly."

Slash smiled, but Finn didn't notice. "Of course. Sorry. Nonetheless, as X-Corp's Director of Information Security, this is your call."

"What about Ben?" I referred to Ben Steinhouser, who co-founded X-Corp with Finn and used to work at the National Security Agency just like I once did. He's a living legend among hackers, programmers and cryptanalysts. I basically lived in awe of him.

"Ben's caught something else," Finn replied. "Besides, his hacking methods are a bit out-of-date. Not that he couldn't catch up if given the time, but time seems to be of the essence here."

"You mean we have *another* client?" In the past few months since X-Corp opened its door, we'd had only one case. Then in one day, we suddenly had two.

Finn nodded, but didn't elaborate. That put us back to square one, with me looking at Slash and him watching me back with smoky, mysterious brown eyes.

"Sure. I'm game."

Slash stood and shook hands with Finn. "I'll be back in half an hour to sign the paperwork. *Cara*, I'll pick you up in two hours. Pack a suitcase and your passport. I'll bring the equipment. Have one of your assistants enable your phone for international calling and texting."

Finn handed Slash some papers. "Don't worry, Slash. We'll help your uncle and be discreet."

Not that I'm paranoid or anything, but as soon as he said the word discreet, both men turned to stare at me.

I lifted my hands. "Hey, discreet is my middle name."

Finn looked away and Slash shook his head as he left the office. I tried not to be too insulted. Then, for a moment, I just let it all sink in. I inhaled a deep breath and let it out slowly.

Oh. My. God.

I was going to Rome.

Chapter Three

Before I could start dancing a jig, Finn hugged me. “How are you, Lexi?”

“I’m stunned, of course. We have two new cases and I’m going to Rome.”

“Are you sure you’re okay with this?”

“Are you?”

He paused, his eyes searching mine. “I’ve missed you. My family is driving me bonkers. Thank God they leave tomorrow.”

“It was nice of them to visit.” Finn’s parents had surprised him (and me) by showing up at Finn’s house just as I was about to take a shower. To make a long story short, his entire family saw me naked and I hadn’t even been introduced to them yet. What might have happened afterward between Finn and I remains a mystery because just as soon as I got dressed, I hightailed it the heck out of his house.

Finn released me and sighed. “They want to meet you.”

“They *already* met me.”

“I mean in a proper way. Like when you aren’t naked.”

“You would have to remind me of that. I’m afraid it

will have to wait until another time, possibly five hundred years in the future."

"Very funny."

"Not really."

Secretly I was relieved I had a good excuse to avoid them because I was nowhere ready to face Finn's family, especially when I was unsure of our relationship and whether we had one or not. Figuring this kind of thing out was definitely not my strong suit.

I looked down at my hands. "Um, Finn, about the shower and why I didn't invite you in with me..."

He put a hand on my shoulder. "You don't have to say or explain anything."

"Yes, I do. I'm just not sure I'm ready for this relationship thing. Not that I'm suggesting we already have a relationship or you even *want* one with me. For all I know, you might be only interested in the sex. After all, it's suggested that 94.6 percent of men's first thought upon seeing a woman for the first time is whether or not they'd like to have sex with her. This makes sense in an evolutionary, biological way, of course. Not that I'm opposed to having sex with you. In fact, it interests me a lot. I like you and I think we would probably be compatible at sex. However, because you're also my boss it adds a layer of complexity to the potential relationship, or non-relationship, that I'm not sure I'm ready to handle. I need to think about things."

Finn just stared at me and then chuckled. "God, I'll miss you, Lexi."

"You will?"

He smiled and I liked the way his eyes crinkled at the corners. "I will. Stop overthinking. We'll talk over things when you get back. Okay? And just so you know, it's not all about the sex with you."

I let out a sigh of relief. He didn't seem to hate me, nor did he seem ready to fire me. But now I wondered if he even wanted to have sex with me anymore. Jeez, why was it all so confusing?

He nudged my chin up. "Be safe in Rome, okay?"

I nodded. "And discreet. I didn't miss the way you gave me that pointed look."

He laughed. "Yes, be especially discreet. Don't forget you still owe me a birthday present."

I picked up my laptop. "Yeah, well, I'm working on that."

"As soon as you get back from Rome, it's dinner at my place and we can have our talk."

"Didn't we already try dinner at your place once and it ended in disaster?"

"Well, this time there will be homemade clam linguine, vintage wine and no after-dinner surprise guests."

"Promises, promises."

"Bloody right, I'm promising. I'll hire security guards, if necessary."

"Okay. I'll look forward to it, then."

We left the conference room together and I headed toward my office. I didn't think I'd need anything but my laptop and some cables and special outlet plugs for Europe. Undoubtedly Slash would have much more sophisticated equipment at his disposal, probably all of it unregistered and untraceable. I instructed one of my assistants to take care of the international calling for my phone and headed out.

I drove home and quickly packed a suitcase. Since I didn't think I'd be going to the opera, I packed mostly jeans, sweaters, nice slacks and a couple of blouses.

I tucked my passport in my purse along with my cell phone and charger and I was ready.

Slash picked me up shortly thereafter and we drove to the airport in his fancy black SUV. Two matching SUV's trailed close behind us.

I glanced in the passenger side rear-view mirror. "Who are they?"

"The FBI."

"Bald Eagle?"

Slash sighed. "I'm sorry I had to leave the opera so unexpectedly, *cara*. My uncle contacted me from the police station where he was being questioned. He was quite distraught."

"Understandably so."

"You left me a rose?"

"You were already sleeping. Soundly." He glanced sideways at me. "I don't typically leave a woman unattended when she's with me."

"You didn't leave me unattended. You sent me Baldy."

"That's not what I meant."

"He was nice even though he wouldn't tell me if your name is Giovanni or not."

"I already told you it's not."

"Okay then, what is it?"

"Slash."

I sighed. "Okay, I get it. You're not at liberty to tell me. But if I figure it out…"

He grinned and gunned the engine, causing the FBI to scramble to keep up.

We didn't talk for the rest of the way to the airport. Not that I was one for small talk anyway and Slash seemed distracted about his uncle. Luckily for us, it was a companionable silence. We were good together in that way. More than once Slash looked my way and it seemed his face, all hard and chiseled angles, seemed to relax. Maybe he did have a soft spot for me after all.

It didn't take us long to arrive at the airport, but we didn't approach the main terminal, rather a smaller one adjacent to the airfield. Slash had arranged a private jet to take us to Italy. I guess when you are a national treasure the paycheck is pretty darn impressive. As I'd never ridden on a private jet before, I was suitably impressed.

"What happens to the FBI now? Do they follow in a surveillance plane?"

Slash laughed. "No, *cara*. They will not follow me to Italy. There are other ways they can keep track of me."

I didn't know what that meant, and it looked like he wasn't going to tell me—top secret and all—so I let it drop.

Slash and I were the only two people on the plane other than the flight crew and two attractive attendants. I felt like a queen as Slash insisted on plying me with champagne, orange juice and a delicious spread of pastries and finger sandwiches.

"Jeez, this is better than a five-star hotel." I stuffed my mouth with a tuna ball wrapped in cheese.

Slash dipped his champagne glass toward the window. "The view is quite spectacular, as well."

"Agreed."

After I'd eaten my fill, which was most everything, I leaned back in my chair to digest. Slash sipped his champagne and stared out the window. At some point I asked him for more information on his uncle's situation. He reached into his briefcase and pulled out a totally chic laptop. He fired it up and pulled up a document.

I scooted over closer, leaning in next to him. I didn't

know what aftershave or soap he used, but he always smelled good.

Slash tapped a spot on a spreadsheet. "There have been two transfers of funds with my uncle's so-called approval to an offshore bank in Bali. They happened over a period of twenty-four hours. The two withdrawals were for nine million euros each. Total amount of money missing—eighteen million euros."

I whistled. "No red flags went up?"

"The withdrawals were disguised to look like legit transfers to approved clients with my uncle's okay. Only they never got the money. It went to the account in Bali. He was lucky he noticed so quickly."

"Hmm. What constitutes your uncle's approval?"

"Digital codes. Virtual keys. This would be a very intricate hack."

"It smacks to me of an inside job."

"Agreed. All the more reason we must be discreet."

I didn't want to think about the political or religious fallout of a scandal of this magnitude. Luckily, I was the tech person, so my job was to figure out who did it and how. I'd leave all that other damage control to the experts.

We talked a bit more about the case, but since neither of us had enough information yet it was just speculative. Still, there was something relaxing and enjoyable about being able to tech-speak for an hour or two with someone without having to stop for all the explanations. Plus, there was the fact that Slash had casually draped his arm around me. After a while, I began to feel light-headed. Whether it was from the constant stream of champagne or his intoxicating scent, I wasn't sure.

I must have fallen asleep because the next thing I know I opened my eyes and realized my head had fallen on his shoulder. Slash was sleeping, too. His mouth, slightly open, rested against my hair, his breath warming my scalp. His arm remained around me, his elegant hacker fingers lightly tangled in my shirt. Someone, probably a flight attendant, had draped a blanket over both of us and discreetly retreated. I tried to move away, but his arm tightened around me and he mumbled against my hair.

I was saved from doing anything else when he began to stir. As if on cue, the flight attendant magically appeared with fresh fruit and coffee. Slash yawned and stretched and the second he did, I shifted safely away, embarrassed that I had cuddled up with him. Were friends supposed to snuggle? Technically, since nothing had happened (I think), I probably worried over nothing. Slash didn't appear to be concerned in the slightest, so I took that as a good sign that nothing was the answer.

I made a quick trip to the bathroom and so did Slash. Afterwards, we sat chatting more about the case while sipping coffee. I also asked a lot of questions about Italy since I'd never been there. Even though I'd be working, I was excited. I'd be in Rome, after all. Slash spoke a lot about Italy, but very little about his family except to say they didn't live in the city.

The time passed quickly. Soon we were landing in Rome and then Slash and I were whisked through customs. Slash knew some of the guys because he laughed and chatted with them as they performed a very cursory look at all our equipment. A driver met us as we came out of customs, helped load our luggage and considerable computer equipment into the car, and drove us to our hotel. I craned my neck out the window the entire time, looking at the beautiful scenery and historical buildings.

The car stopped in front of an old, ornate structure with a sign that read *Hotel Atlante Star.*

I climbed out of the car, gazing around in awe. The location was amazing. "Wow. Is that St. Peter's Basilica over there?"

"*Si*, it's the gateway to the Vatican, *cara.* We're right downtown, between San Pietro and the River Tiber."

"It's stunning."

"It is." Slash got out, slipping his laptop case over his shoulder and helping the driver unload the trunk. "We're just a three-minute walk to the Vatican."

I went inside to get a trolley to cart our stuff to the room. Slash checked us in quickly and declined the aid of a bellhop. I didn't blame him. I wouldn't trust anyone else to my computer equipment either. We rode the elevator to the fourth floor and Slash opened the doors to a beautiful suite. It had a large living area with ornate furniture and glass doors that opened to a tiny balcony overlooking the street. You could see St. Peter's Basilica from the window.

I held the suite doors open while Slash rolled in the trolley with our stuff. "The suite has two similar rooms. I'll take the one to the right."

I grabbed my suitcase and walked to the left-side room. It had a large four-poster bed, a heavy dresser and desk. Red velvet curtains hung at the window, tapestries adorned the walls, and gold and red bedspread completed the look. I whistled. Seriously nice digs.

Pulling my suitcase into the room, I dumped most of the contents into a couple of drawers. I hung the few blazers and blouses I'd brought in a fancy wooden wardrobe and tucked the suitcase away beneath the bed.

I had just visited the attached bathroom when I heard Slash talking to someone out in the common area. Sweeping my hair back into a ponytail, I went to see who'd arrived.

Slash was setting up our computer equipment on several tables he'd pushed together. He spoke in what sounded like German to a tall, muscular guy with military-cut brown hair, dressed in jeans and a black sweater. I could only see the back of his head.

Slash glanced over my way. "Come here, Lexi."

The stranger turned as I approached them. The first thing I noticed about him is that he had the most beautiful green eyes I'd ever seen.

"Lexi, meet Tito Blickensderfer. Tito, this is Lexi Carmichael."

"Blickensderfer?"

Tito stuck out a hand and I shook it. "It's a Swiss name."

"You're from Switzerland?"

Slash crawled out from beneath the table. "He's a member of the Swiss Guard."

"You mean the Pope's bodyguards at the Vatican?"

"*Si*. Tito and I go way back."

I noticed the gold chain that hung from Tito's neck and knew that Slash had a similar one tucked beneath his shirt. I wondered about the origins of their friendship, but didn't have the social wherewithal to ask.

"Were you speaking German?" I asked instead.

Tito nodded. "Yah. I speak Italian, too, but Nico is pretty good with the mother tongue."

I glanced at Slash. "Nico?"

Slash shrugged.

Tito handed Slash another cable and asked, "When do you see your uncle?"

"In a couple of hours. Lexi and I need to finish setting up our equipment and maybe take a nap, so we're fresh."

Tito gave me a strange look and my cheeks heated. I realized the nap comment sounded intimate, like we'd be taking it together. Jeez.

"Yah, okay. I'll come back later. Good luck and keep me posted."

Slash came out from behind the computers and shook his hand before the two guys gave each other a hard hug.

Tito spoke to Slash in German. "*Sicher sein.*"

Slash nodded. After Tito left I asked Slash what he'd said.

"He told me to be safe."

"Are you in danger?"

Slash smiled. "With you around, always."

I wasn't sure if it was a joke or not, so I didn't laugh.

He patted me on the arm. "Let's finish setting up, *cara*, and then we can have a bit of downtime to relax. I want us to be clear-headed when we meet my uncle."

He didn't mention anything about napping together so I breathed a sigh of relief. Perhaps Tito had warned Slash to be safe, but every time he was around me, my senses went on high alert.

The more pressing question was: Who was in danger from whom?

Chapter Four

We met Slash's uncle, Benedetto De Luca, in the afternoon after both Slash and I had taken a good three-hour nap. I still felt weirded out, jet lagged and had a bit of a stomachache, but I played the good trooper. A bank worker dressed in a three-piece suit led us to a large office adorned with heavy antique pieces of furniture, including an enormous, ornate desk. The walls were paneled in wood and the carpet felt plush beneath my tennis shoes. When we entered, a tall dark-haired man with a mustache and a worried expression rose from behind the desk and came around to greet us.

"Stefano." He gave Slash a big hug and then a kiss on each cheek. He murmured something in Italian to which Slash replied by nodding and patting his arm. Slash turned his uncle toward me.

"This is Lexi Carmichael. She is working for X-Corp, the company I hired to help with your situation. She's a good person to have on our side and is a personal friend as well."

There it was—we *were* friends. *Personal* friends even.

Benedetto turned his gaze on me, a dark eyebrow lifting as he mentally assessed whether I was up to the challenge.

"If you are a friend of Stefano's, then you are family while you are here. I am grateful for your assistance"

"Ah, no problem." I hoped this was the right response.

"Sit down, please."

Slash helped me out of my coat as Benedetto went to a small refrigerator and opened it. "May I offer you water, coffee or something else to drink?"

"Water would be great." I glanced over at Slash. "Would you like some, too, *Stefano*?"

Slash smiled and took a bottle. We sat, ready to hear his story. It was little different from what Slash had already learned except that Benedetto had discovered the fraudulent transfers about forty-eight hours earlier and about seven hours before the police arrived at the bank. The money had been transferred to the same account in Bali and had been cleaned out less than two hours later. All the transfers had been made from Benedetto's account, which was tightly protected.

Benedetto leaned back in his chair. "I assure you, it wasn't me who made those transfers."

I nodded. "I believe you. But you're under suspicion, nonetheless."

"*Si.*"

"It has to be someone who has access to your account information." I took a sip of water. "Your secretary or personal assistant, perhaps?"

"They have my account information, but not my passwords."

"Sorry for asking, but what would happen if you got hit by a bus? Who would be able to get access to your account?"

"The passwords are locked in the bank vault, accessible only to the Bank President, Donatello Ferrari."

I glanced at Slash. "Ferrari? Like the car?"

Slash shrugged. "It's a popular surname in Italy."

"What about the IT team?"

Benedetto looked puzzled. Slash said something quickly in Italian and Benedetto shook his head. "No, no. They could re-set the system, but I would be informed and new passwords would have to be instituted by me. I got no such notification and I did not create new passwords. It is a mystery."

I thought for a moment. "It's got to be from the inside. We're going to have to hack the hacker."

Slash didn't look surprised, but Benedetto looked to Slash for a translation. Slash obliged and Benedetto put his head in his hands.

"*Buo dia*, what do you mean by that?"

"If we are going to find out who hacked into your account, I'm going to have to hack in as well and see if I can run a trace. You should know that whatever I discover, if anything, would be inadmissible in court. What I'm doing isn't exactly legal either, so it has to remain hush-hush. If it's an inside job, which is where I'm leaning, then all we can do is use the information to trip up or trap the hacker in another, more legal way."

Benedetto sighed and said something to Slash in Italian. They spoke for a minute before Benedetto stood. I glanced at Slash.

"He agrees, but says the fewer details he knows the better. Especially the questionable ones."

"Understood."

Benedetto handed me a sheet of paper and then motioned me to his chair. Rising, I went around the desk and sat in his nice leather swivel. He said something else to Slash and then left the office.

I looked down at the paper and realized he had given

me his passwords. "We're going to have to change them ASAP."

"That's a given." Slash came up behind me and rested his hands on my shoulders.

"So, your real name is Stefano."

"No."

"Your uncle called you Stefano."

"It's a running joke in my family. He always got me mixed up with my older brother, Stefano. So, he calls us both Stefano."

"You have an older brother named Stefano?"

"And a younger one, too."

"You have two brothers named Stefano?"

"No, *cara*, the younger brother is Giorgio."

"So, your name is not Stefano."

"No."

"It's not Giorgio?"

"No."

"I really hate that you're enjoying this."

Sighing, I put my fingers on the keyboard and then logged in. Leaning back, I took a few minutes to check out the system, the software and the security. Slash watched me for a moment and then leaned down and kissed the top of my head.

"I'm going to let you take a solo crack at this for now. I've arranged to meet with some old friends who will be able to fill me in on the police investigation so far. After that, I'm going to talk to the bank IT team, see what I can learn about the system from the inside. I'll be back in a bit to help you. You'll be okay?"

"Of course. Thanks for letting me, I mean X-Corp, have first crack. I appreciate it."

He patted my shoulder and left. Taking a deep breath, I sipped my water, flexed my fingers and got to work.

I loved this part, despite the fact that my stomach was jangling. Hacking into the Vatican's Bank from the inside was certainly an once-in-a-lifetime experience. Something to tell the grandkids, I suppose, that is if I ever managed to have sex more than once, let alone kids.

After the first hour I lost track of time. Whoever had hacked Benedetto's account was good. Very good. I couldn't find a trace signature anywhere. Yet something bothered me. It was spectacular, innovative hack, but…flashy. It drew attention. Benedetto knew nothing about hacking and even he'd been able to discover it quickly. There were a hundred different things I would have done to better disguise the hack. Simple things. Yet, he'd left it out in the open. He'd done a good job hiding the trail, so why the heck send a blinking neon light advertising the hack in the first place? Technically I guess it didn't matter. The hack had served its purpose and the money was gone. Still, something felt off. My hacker senses were tingling. I just couldn't put my fingers on it, literally or figuratively.

Worse, I still couldn't trace the hack. After several lengthy maneuvers that got me exactly nowhere, I sat back to re-think my approach. I had to think like the hacker who'd broken in, not like someone who was trying to find him. After a minute, I started typing again. This time I started making a bit of headway.

After what had to be at least another hour, I muttered under my breath. "You sneaky noob. Where are you?"

It took another hour, maybe two. Finally, I found a thread. I leaned back in my chair and grinned. Once I had a thread, there was no stopping me. True to form, in minutes the entire hack unraveled.

I had him.

My fingers flew over the keyboard, searching the bank database until it led me right to the terminal I needed. I copied the terminal number and then tagged it to find the user.

Bingo. My trace had been perfect except I'd been wrong on one front. The hacker hadn't been a he. It was a she.

Her name was Serafina Lino and she was the Assistant Comp Controller for European Accounts. I pulled out my cell phone and texted Slash that I'd found our hacker or at least the terminal where the hack had originated. I stood, stretched and got a bottle of water from Bendetteto's fridge, realizing I was ravenously hungry. My phone beeped and I checked the text. It was from Slash and said Serafina hadn't shown up for work this morning. I should proceed to her office and he'd have Benedetto clear me to have access to her computer. Still holding the bottle of water, I exited the office and asked one of the secretaries in which direction to head to find the office. I stopped for a bathroom break and wished there was a vending machine handy. Guess the Vatican Bank wasn't big on Pepsi and processed crackers.

It turned out that Serafina's office wasn't an office at all, but a small cubicle. The chair was empty and the computer had been turned off. I poked my head into the next cubicle where a young man studied an impressive spreadsheet on a large color monitor.

"Excuse me. Do you speak English?"

He turned around in his chair and fiddled with the glasses that had slid down his nose. "Oh, yes. I do. Are you the lady with the *policia*?"

"Uh, not exactly. I'm Lexi Carmichael. Mr. Benedetto was supposed to okay me taking a look at Ms. Lino's computer."

He swiveled back to his desk and picked up a small notepad. "*Si,* Mr. Benedetto just called. He says computer people fix password for you." He handed me a slip of paper on which was written *A62x4P.*

"Please go ahead and have her computer. Do tell me if you have any road kills or errors."

He looked so proud of himself for being able to conduct himself in English, I didn't have the heart to correct him. Besides, it wasn't like I was even giving Italian a shot.

"Well, thanks. Um, did Miss Lino call in sick today?"

He shrugged. "Don't know. She no call at all."

"Is she sick a lot?"

"Oh, no. Serafina a good girl. Work hard."

"Did you have a power outage or anything like that lately?"

He looked at me puzzled, so I tried again. "No power last night or today?" I went to the outlet and pretended to pull the cord. "No electricity?"

"Oh, no. No problems."

Something niggled at me. "Do you typically shut down your computer at the end of each day?"

"No. We must leave on for backed up."

"Interesting. Thanks."

I sat down in Serafina's chair and waited while the computer booted up. Her desk was neat with a box of tissues, a little jar of peppermint candies and a photo of a middle-aged couple.

I walked back over to her neighbor. "Sorry to bother you again. Is Serafina a young woman or old?"

"Young?"

"You know, my age?"

"Ah. Yes. She young. No married and no bambinos."

"Okay, thanks." That probably meant the picture on

her desk was her parents. I studied them, thinking they looked ordinary and happy. Guess they wouldn't be so thrilled when they heard their daughter had been arrested for hacking into the bank.

By the time I got back, the computer was up and running. I entered Serafina's user name and password and I was in. I did a cursory look around, checked out the system she was running and the main application software. Then I started a more methodical search. It took me less than a minute to find the program for which I'd been looking. Serafina had openly planted a gateway program allowing remote access to the files inside the system. After she opened and executed the program, she'd provided a wide open door for a hacker or hackers to waltz right in and set up shop.

"What were you thinking, Serafina?" I murmured.

A quick glance through the rest of the system told me several other things. Serafina herself was not a hacker. She'd been either tricked or paid well to plant the program. Someone with far more sophistication had used the gateway to begin a series of spectacular hacks to access and transfer the money from Bendetteto's account and then hide the trail.

I opened random other files, but not surprisingly most everything was either a spreadsheet or written in Italian. I ran a protocol and discovered three unusual and encrypted files. I copied them and the gateway program onto the flash drive on my key chain and then shut down. There was nothing else for me to find here. Standing, I stretched and asked Serafina's colleague for her address and phone number. He provided it and I thanked him and stepped to a quiet corner. I texted Slash about what I'd discovered and suggested we stop by Serafina's apartment to talk to her. A minute later,

Slash texted back that he was in a meeting, but would send someone else to take me. He gave me instructions where to wait in front of the bank and then said he'd try to meet me at her apartment as soon as he could.

I retrieved my coat and exited the bank, grateful to have a moment of fresh air and sunshine. I marveled at the historic beauty of the architecture around me and then sat on a bench near the fountain Slash had indicated. Pigeons were everywhere. It was crazy. People were feeding them pieces of bread and other things. They strolled right up to me, unafraid, but didn't stick around long when they realized I didn't have any food.

After a few minutes an extremely small dark blue Fiat drove up and honked at me. I stood, walking toward the car. Tito had somehow squeezed behind the wheel.

"Hey, Tito." I climbed in. "Thanks for coming."

"No problem."

"Don't you have guard duties? Protecting the Pope and all that?"

"It's my day off."

"You know, I'd really like to see you in those colorful guard pantaloons some time."

He looked sideways at me. "That's our dress uniform. We don't wear it all that often."

"I'm still hopeful I'll see it."

"Being hopeful is a godly pursuit."

"Good to know."

I rattled off Serafina's address and he punched it into his GPS. "Did Slash fill you in?"

"Yah. He says she may know something about his uncle's troubles."

"She may be the *source* of his uncle's trouble."

He gave me a grin. "You work fast. I see why Nico likes you."

"It's just a first step. By the way, why do you call him Nico?"

Tito shrugged. "It's better than calling him idiot."

Guess he had a point.

Tito drove slowly and we looked at the building numbers until we found Serafina's. It was a three-story stone building next to a lovely white brick church with a black spire and grassy courtyard.

Tito pulled up on the sidewalk and shut off the ignition.

"Is this a legal parking spot?"

He got out of the car. Shrugging, I followed suit. An elderly lady carrying two plastic bags was just coming out the front door to the building. Tito caught the door for her, holding it open. She went out and we went in.

I dug in my pocket to find the scrap of paper where I'd written her address. "She's in apartment number 302."

We climbed the stairs to the third floor and down the short hall until we came to room 302. The door was ajar.

"Serafina Lino?" Tito knocked and then pushed the door open wider with his elbow.

There was no answer.

I glanced at Tito. "I'm going out on a limb here and say this isn't a good sign."

Tito stepped inside, motioning for me to follow. There was a small kitchen to the right and a living area straight ahead. He took a quick peek into both but shook his head. He motioned down a small corridor where presumably the bedroom was located.

I took one step into the corridor after him and knew there was trouble.

The smell nearly knocked me over.

Tito knew it, too, because he grabbed my hand and squeezed it.

Tito called out again, but even I knew it was pointless. We crept down the small corridor for what seemed like forever, past a tiny bathroom and into the bedroom.

That's where we found Serafina lying on the bed.

She was very, very dead.

Chapter Five

I felt the gorge rise in my throat. Her throat had been slashed and there was blood everywhere.

I pressed a hand against my mouth as Tito grabbed my arm and pulled me out of the bedroom.

"*Mio Dio.* We have to call Nico at once."

"Are you completely nuts? We have to call the *police*. That's a dead body in there."

Tito shook his head. "Nico first. We have to handle this carefully."

The gorge rose again and I battled it back. "Tito, it's not like I want to alarm you, but we've moved *way* past careful."

Footsteps sounded behind us and I jumped. Slash put a hand on my shoulder.

"Tito is right, *cara.* We must be careful. Next time, close the door behind you, my friends."

"Slash. Oh, my God. Serafina. She's dead."

Slash stepped into the bedroom, took a quick look, and then came back out again. He pulled us toward the kitchen. "We've got to get out of here."

I started hyperventilating. "What is *wrong* with you guys? We are talking about a dead body. We've got to call the police. Someone murdered her."

"*Si*, but it wasn't us. Did you touch anything?"

Tito and I shook our heads.

"Good. We'll call the police, *cara*. Anonymously. The red tape of being involved in an international homicide investigation would tie us up unnecessarily. You've got to trust me. If we figure out what she was into, we'll catch her murderer. But not if we are hampered by the *policia*." Slash looked around. "We aren't going to find anything left of use here anyway."

I followed his gaze and for the first time realized that the place was trashed. Someone, perhaps the person who had killed Serafina, had been looking for something. Drawers were emptied, books, papers, and knickknacks littered the floor. Couch and chair cushions had been ripped open and stuffing strewn across the floor.

I kept remembering how Serafina looked lying on her bed with her throat slit and the blood all over the white bedspread and I felt my stomach heave again.

Maybe Slash sensed I was about to hurl because he took my arm and we exited the apartment, followed closely by Tito, who closed the door and wiped the knob clean. Luckily the hallway was empty, but we hadn't been careful when we arrived. There was no telling who had seen us, in addition to the elderly lady for whom Tito had held the door. My stomach still felt queasy and I'm pretty sure my face resembled Casper the Ghost's. I felt significantly better once we were out on the sidewalk having a breath of fresh air.

Slash put an arm around me, letting me rest my head on his shoulder. "Are you all right, *cara?*"

"Not exactly."

"I'm sorry. It was a bad idea to permit you to visit her."

"It was *my* idea, so don't blame yourself."

Tito ran his fingers through his hair. "What have you stumbled onto, my friend?"

Slash frowned. "I'm not certain. Yet."

We walked around the corner and Slash took out his cell phone. He spoke rapidly into the phone for a moment and then hung up.

"*Policia?*" Tito asked.

"Someone will call them." Slash returned the phone to his pocket.

Before I could ask him to whom he referred, I heard a voice from behind us.

"Angelico?"

Slash and I turned as a unit and my mouth fell open as the most beautiful woman I had ever seen approached us. She had jet black hair and it fell in a curtain down to her waist. She wore a tight red dress that hugged every inch of her body and a short fur coat. She let off a stream of Italian from a pair of Angelica Jolie-inspired lips and then threw herself into Slash's arms. Seeing as how one of those arms was still around me, I ended up with her pressed against me, too, and pieces of her hair floating into my open mouth.

Sputtering, I disentangled myself. I was getting pretty darn sick of being smashed by women who threw themselves at Slash.

The two of them began a rapid conversation in Italian while I stood next to Tito and watched. The woman spoke in a very animated fashion with her hands waving around while Slash listened, slightly amused, his arms crossed against his chest. Finally, he put a hand on her arm and pulled her over to us.

"Lexi, meet Bianca. She's an old friend of mine."

I lifted an eyebrow. "You have a lot of friends for a guy who doesn't have many friends."

Slash smiled, while Bianca gave me a head-to-toe perusal. "Lexi? That's an interesting name."

The way she said it implied that she didn't think it was interesting at all, but somehow distasteful.

She linked arms with Slash. "So, Lexi, how do you know our Angelico?"

I narrowed my eyes at Slash. This was the second time in as many days as I had been asked this question and I didn't like how it had turned out the last time. This time, I chose my words carefully and kept my distance.

"Um, *Angelico* and I are friends from work. Sort of."

Apparently considering me less than worthy of her attention, she dismissed me and turned to Tito, her expression warming. "*Ciao*, Tito." She held out a hand to him and he lifted it to his mouth and kissed it.

I thought back to my first meeting with Tito. He'd shaken my hand, not kissed my knuckles. Why didn't I rate a kiss on the hand? What was wrong with my knuckles?

Police cars suddenly screamed up the street and Slash said something in Italian to Bianca. She looked over her shoulder and after a quick peck on his cheek, took off.

Slash turned to me and took my arm. "Time to go, *cara*. We'll take my car. Tito can come back later and retrieve his." He steered me toward a black sedan parked a few blocks away. I climbed into the front passenger seat and Tito in the back. Slash did a U-turn and we headed back to the hotel.

I sat in the car with my arms crossed against my chest. I felt drained, sick and grumpy. "Did you tell Bianca about … Serafina?" I asked Slash.

He shook his head. "No, *cara*. That's our secret. She knows only that I'm trying to help my uncle. She heard

I was in town. In was coincidental that we ran into each other."

I wasn't a big believer in coincidence, but I held my tongue. "Lucky us. So, what's next, *Angelico*?"

Tito laughed from the back seat. "Ah, Lexi. His name isn't Angelico either. He always gives women a different name. Makes it easier to love them and leave them."

"Ha, ha. Very funny. Doesn't it bother you that you don't know his real name?"

Tito shrugged. "Not really. But I have to call him something, yah? Nico works fine."

Slash's mouth twitched with a smile.

Tito stretched his legs out, his knees pressing against the back of my seat. "So, my friend of many names, have you seen Bianca since SISMI?"

Slash shook his head slightly.

"What's SISMI?" I asked.

Tito leaned forward. "The Italian version of the CIA."

My eyebrow shot up. "Bianca was in the CIA?"

Tito snorted. "She's still in as far as I know. She's a secret weapon of her own making. I'm sure the Motherland owes her a great debt."

Slash's lips twitched again and for some reason that made me crankier. Didn't anyone care we'd just found a dead body? Maybe this was an everyday occurrence for these guys, but it was pretty darn awful for me. I just stared out the window until we reached the hotel.

As soon as we were inside, I went to take a shower. I threw my clothes in the trash. I would never, *ever* wear them again. They would always remind me of Serafina Lino. Just thinking about her made my stomach queasy. I sat on the top of the toilet seat until I was sure I wouldn't hurl. Finally I ran the water as hot as

I could stand and scrubbed every inch of my body. It didn't really help. I kept seeing her lying there on the bed and wondered if I'd ever get past it.

When I came out, Slash and Tito were on the balcony drinking coffee and speaking in low voices. They both looked up when they saw me.

Slash stood, walked over to me. Without a word, he hugged me. "I'm sorry, *cara*. I'm sorry you had to see that."

"It's okay. You didn't know. I didn't know. This was supposed to be about hacking, not murder."

"Come sit."

I sat at the table on the balcony. Slash handed me a glass of water and Tito studied me with his green eyes. "You held up pretty good back there for a novice."

Slash nodded. "She's tough." He ran his fingers through his hair and sighed. "You should know *cara*, that sometimes in our line of work, we see unpleasant things. Ugly things. We all have coping mechanisms. Sometimes we use humor, sometimes we don't. I want you to understand that it is, in no way, a sign of disrespect. We *will* find out who murdered Serafina. I give you my word."

I nodded, threaded my fingers together on top of the table. "I realize that. I'm okay, Slash. Really. I just got shook up a bit. I get what needs to be done here. I'm back in the game. Time is of the essence."

Slash put his hand on top of mine. "Benedetto says the police are already at the bank confiscating Serafina's computer and files. Can you think of anything you might have seen on her hard drive that might help us?"

"Well, sure I saw lots of stuff, mostly spreadsheets. I didn't have time to review it all."

Tito sighed. "Too bad we couldn't get another look at it."

"We can."

I went back into my room and retrieved my keychain. I disconnected the flash drive and carried it back out to the balcony. "At least we can look at some of them. I took three heavily encrypted files she had hidden and the gateway program that initiated the hack."

Slash stood up so quickly he almost upended the table. "You copied files? I thought you were only taking a look."

I gave him a sheepish smile. "Whoops."

"No, *cara*, you are brilliant."

He came around the table and kissed me hard on the mouth. After he released me, I realized my head was spinning. Whether from the kiss or the compliment, I'm not sure. Embarrassed, I glanced over at Tito, but he was staring out at the plaza, apparently not thinking it a big deal that Slash had just planted a huge one on me. Given his nonchalant reaction, I took it to mean it was not a significant male gesture despite my pounding heart. Nonetheless, there was an awful lot of kissing going on lately. Hands, cheeks and mouth. I guess it was some kind of Italian thing. Seeing as how I would be in Italy for an extended period of time, I supposed I'd better get used to it, although it sure did confuse the heck out of me.

Slash took my flash drive to our small command and control center. He plugged the drive into one of the laptops while Tito and I watched over his shoulder.

"Any file in particular stand out to you, *cara?*"

"This one for sure." I pointed at it. "Don't know what *quadro* means, but it was all alone in a folder buried in two other folders. I did a standard search for cryppies and three files came up. For some reason the way she'd planted this one seemed odd to me. Amateur, but odd."

"Painting," he murmured.

"Is that what *quadro* means?"

"Hmmm..." He began initiating a routine to crack the encryption. It wouldn't be easy, but with the high-end hardware Slash had brought with him, added to the hacking experience between the two of us, at least we had a fighting chance. Once that one was underway, he started similar routines on the other files and leaned back in the chair. This would take some time.

"Now what?" I asked.

"Now we should learn all we can about Serafina Lino. I'll head back to the bank to find out about her first-hand from my uncle and her co-workers. You can call Finn and fill him in on our progress. Then you've earned some down time, *cara*."

I shook my head. "No. I'd rather work. Really."

He looked doubtful, but didn't argue. "Alright. If you're up to it, see what you can find about Serafina online. Tito will help you overcome any translation barriers."

Slash left and I retreated to my room to call Finn and bring him up-to-date. It was early morning in Washington and I caught him on the way into the office. I gave him the short and sanitized version of what happened, leaving out the part about finding the dead body. I didn't tell him for two reasons. One, I didn't know how secure my phone was and two, I didn't want to re-live the experience while it was still fresh. Finn seemed satisfied with our progress and I promised to call him again soon. I sensed that he wanted to talk more, but he got another call and had to take it. I was kind of relieved to hang up because so much had happened to me in these past two days that I didn't really feel like chatting about it yet.

I returned to the living room and sat down in front of one of the laptops. Tito was already busy on another one. We worked for a while in companionable silence.

Part of the reason I loved hacking was that I could lose all connection to the real world. Sometimes I had trouble navigating the real world. My virtual world was my zen, my center. I needed to get back to that for a while. Besides, right now, banishing the image of Serafina lying in the bed with her throat slit took precedent over everything else. I didn't even *want* to think about what my dreams might be like.

As a result of my unusual focus, it took me mere minutes to obtain the information on Serafina's date and place of her birth, weight, height and eye color, and how many brothers, sisters, nephews and nieces she had. I learned her parents lived in a small town about thirty minutes south of Rome. Her mother was the principal of a local high school and her father a power broker. Serafina had gone to Sapienza University of Rome and majored in accounting. She had no criminal record and was free of any outstanding debts. I peeked into her two social media accounts and discovered she had zillions of friends. To my enormous relief, I was able to pass off the responsibility of reading through her posts to Tito since they were in Italian. I barely cared about my own social life. Being forced to read about someone else's held as much appeal as a lobotomy.

After about an hour, Tito leaned back in his chair and rubbed his neck. "She's been dating someone named Marcus."

"For how long?"

He shook his head. "Looks like maybe four or five months. They met online through a dating service."

"Marcus doesn't sound very Italian."

"German, actually. Possibly Swiss. Hard to say."

My fingers poised over the keyboard. "Got a last name?"

"No, and there's no Marcus in her friend list."

I thought for a moment. "Does she mention the dating service she used? Maybe we can track him down from there."

He went back and started reading again. "Don't see it yet, but she posted an amazing picture of gnocchi."

"Who's that?"

He glanced up at me. "Gnocchi? It's a food, not a who."

"She posted a picture of food?"

Tito nodded. "It looks incredible. She must have been a good cook. Now I'm hungry."

"I don't get it. Why would anyone post a picture of their dinner?" I certainly didn't want the world to know I usually ate cereal for dinner.

He shrugged. "Why not?"

I didn't say anything. Clearly the social media frontier was way too complex for me to fathom at this stage of my life.

Tito went back to reading and I checked on the progress of the encryption programs and saw that exactly diddley progress on the suspect file had been made despite the high caliber of hardware and software Slash was running. However, we were having better luck on some of the other files and at least two looked ready to crack.

"Okay, I've got it," Tito said. "*Amore a Prima Vista.*"

"In English?"

"Loosely translated it means 'Love at First Sight. It's the name of the online dating service."

I sat down, my fingers resting on the keyboard. "Can you spell it for me?"

It took me about seven minutes to hack in to the system and another fifteen to go through the long list of clients.

"There are forty-seven clients with the first name of Marcus and seventeen that have it as a last name. Do you know they have over six thousand clients?" The thought of six thousand people all wanting to date each other seemed unfathomable.

I wound my hair into a ponytail and tied it back with a rubber band lying on the table. "Can you give me any more clues, Tito? Did she post a picture of him, mention his age, how he looked, or his hometown?"

He sighed. "Lexi, I'm a man. I can't think on an empty stomach. Can you order some gnocchi from room service while I look? Get coffee, too."

I stood and stretched. Walking over to the phone, I dialed room service and ordered two plates of gnocchi and coffee. I went to the bathroom, checked the status of the encryption programs and got some fresh air on the balcony while Tito continued to read.

Room service and Slash arrived at the same time.

"Gnocchi?" Slash said handing the waiter a tip and lifting a cover from one of the plates.

I eyed the food over his shoulder. "It's a long story, but it smells good."

Slash shook his head. "It will be infinitely inferior to Nonna's gnocchi."

"Nonna?"

Tito came over to the cart, grabbing a plate and some

silverware. "His grandmother. Haven't you ever had gnocchi, Lexi?"

I peered closer at the food. "I don't think so." How could I be sure? It wasn't as if I ever paid close attention to what I ate. Maybe I'd eaten gnocchi a hundred times before and didn't even know it.

Taking a fork, I stabbed it into the little roll. I bit into it and chewed. "Mmmmm...good."

Slash took my fork, skewered a piece of his own and popped it in his mouth. "Not even close." He set the fork down. "So, what did you find out about Serafina Lino?"

I took another bite. "Not much. Other than her vital statistics, we know she studied accounting at a university here in Rome, is the youngest of three brothers and one sister, likes to cook gnocchi and had recently started dating some guy named Marcus she met via an online dating service. We're working on the dating service angle now. How about you?"

Slash poured a cup of coffee, handed it to me and got himself another mug. "The police have confiscated Serafina's computer and work files. Because her place was wrecked and there was no obvious evidence of a sexual attack, her death is currently being classified as a homicide as a possible result of a burglary gone badly. But that will soon change."

"Why?"

"The police want to talk to you. Serafina's co-worker told them about you."

I took a sip and coughed. Slash patted me on the back. My eyes watered. "Jeez. Is this coffee or gasoline?"

Slash smiled. "Italians like their coffee strong."

I'm quite sure you could have started my car with it, but I didn't want to hurt anyone's feelings, so I kept my mouth shut.

I looked around for the cream and sugar. "Okay, so we know the police will find out that I linked Serafina to the hack in Benedetto's computer." I lifted the lid off the sugar bowl and dumped in four heaping teaspoons, considered a fifth. "I'm okay with that, I guess. It's all official X-Corp business, although I'm not providing the particulars on the hack because officially I didn't hack. I explored. Should I tell them I copied some files off her drive?"

"Better not, *cara*. They will be embarrassed enough that in a few hours you managed to do what their team of experts failed to discover over several days. Presumably they have the same files. Let them follow the trail in their own way."

I shrugged and poured in as much cream as I could. "Tito, want some coffee?"

"Please. Keep it black."

I admired his courage. Pouring him a cup, I took it over and he handed me his empty plate. "The gnocchi was pretty good, but I've had better."

It tasted delicious to me, so I didn't complain. "Got anything yet on the boyfriend?"

Tito took a sip of the coffee and didn't even flinch. "Possibly. No picture, but she mentions an Austrian town called Feldkirch in relation to him. She refers to Marcus as a boy from a small town."

"Small-town boy," I murmured. Sitting, I hacked back into the dating service database and typed in Marcus and Feldkirch. Up popped a name and a picture.

"Bingo. Marcus Huber, age twenty-nine, originally from Feldkirch, Austria. He works as a pharmacist at the *Pacifica Farmacia* here in Rome, about three kilometers from here. I've got a home address, too." I printed out his photo and the addresses and handed them to Slash who studied them and then put the paper in his pocket.

"I know where the pharmacy is," Tito said. "It's not that far from here. I've been there a couple of times. We can walk."

Slash moved over to the computers to monitor the progress of the encryption programs. "We're almost in on two of them, but we've got little movement on the big one."

"I know, which makes me all the more suspicious." I took a small sip of the coffee and wished I hadn't. It burned a sludge trail down my esophagus. I coughed again and Slash took the coffee away from me.

"Add more cream or abstain."

"Excellent advice."

He rolled his eyes. "Okay, *cara*, your instincts were right. There's something important in this big file. It's specially encrypted. It's got a different kind of protection than the other two. It may be something new. I've not seen anything like it and I've seen just about everything. I'm going to try a different approach."

I stood behind him, admiring his hacking moves and the way his elegant hands played the keyboard like a true master. "Sweet." I whistled as he initiated a new protocol. "Are you going to teach me that?"

He swiveled around in the chair, took my hands. The pupils in his eyes darkened. "Ah, *cara*, there is much I will teach you."

My heart skipped a beat. I wondered if it would be like this every time he touched me. I cleared my throat. "Thanks. I'd appreciate it."

He smiled. "*Si*, you will, *cara*. Appreciate it, that is."

Jeez. There went the pulse rate again.

Slash stood. "Come, my friends. Let's take a walk.

It would be useful to have first crack at Marcus Huber before the *policia* figure out who he is."

"I thought I had to talk to the police."

"You will. All in good time. But let's pay Marcus a visit first."

Tito rose from his chair. "I'm coming, too. If I have to read one more thing about women's shoes and hot glances I'm going to cough up."

"Throw up," I corrected. "Barf, hurl, kiss the porcelain god. Serafina wrote about hot glances? Why?"

"How do I know? Am I a woman?"

"I'm a woman and I don't write about that."

Slash chuckled. "Of course, you don't *cara.* You don't even have a social media account of any kind."

"That's on purpose, you know."

"*Si*, I know."

Tito grabbed the plate with the rest of my gnocchi. "You finished, Lexi? I'm starving."

I motioned for him to eat it. He shoveled it in, then we headed out. Slash took a minute to hang the 'Do Not Disturb' sign on the handle and then fasten a black gadget between the door and the jamb. He stepped back and a little red light on it began flashing.

I peered at it. "What's that? A bomb?" I was only half-joking.

"Extra security. Let's go."

I wasn't going to get a better explanation, so we set off. It was a lovely afternoon in Rome. I took time to clear my head, enjoy the sights and admire the architecture. Slash and Tito didn't rush me and pointed out famous landmarks as we passed. Tito even took a picture of Slash and me in front of a pretty bubbling fountain.

Fifteen minutes later, Slash stopped in front of an off-white building with an ornate wooden door. I glanced up and saw the sign *Pacifica Farmacia.* Tito held the door open for us and we walked in. The place was small and cramped with all kinds of bottles and jars crammed onto wooden shelves, almost like an antique pharmacy might have looked. There were also plenty of contemporary items stacked neatly on white shelves. I recognized nose sprays, cough syrup and aspirin. Still, it didn't look much like a typical American pharmacy.

An older gentleman came out to greet us and Slash went to speak to him while Tito and I browsed the shelves. I picked up a long, thin box with directions in French and studied the picture of what looked like a thermometer.

"Home pregnancy test?" Slash asked from over my shoulder.

"Agggh!" I jumped, dropping the box on the floor. "I was just browsing. But not for that. Jeez."

Slash picked up the box, handing it to me. I tossed it on the shelf like a hot potato.

Slash leaned in close. "The clerk went to get Marcus. He should be out shortly."

I turned around as another older gentleman came out from a room at the back of the store. He walked up to Slash and said something to him in Italian. Tito joined them, listening and the two of them talked for a bit. Slash took a piece of paper out of his pocket and showed it to the man. They spoke for a few minutes and then the man went behind the counter and pulled out some papers and wrote something down, handing the paper to Slash. Slash and Tito shook his hand, then Slash motioned for me to leave.

We huddled on the sidewalk. "So, where's Marcus?"

"That was Marcus."

"Huh?"

"It appears as if Serafina's boyfriend hijacked his name and profession."

"You mean Marcus is bogus?"

"Not exactly."

Slash handed me the paper with the picture and addresses I had printed out.

"He recognized this guy. Said his name was Alex Rogolli and until three days ago, he worked as a night clerk in the pharmacy."

I squinted in the sun. "So Alex stole his co-worker's name and profession for an online dating service?"

Tito shrugged. "So what? Can't be too careful who you date these days."

Slash and I stared at him until he lifted his hands. "Okay. Dead girl. Not so brilliant comment."

Slash took the paper back from me. "Marcus said Alex only worked there a month. Showed up, was pleasant to the customers, and kept the cash register on target. Stayed to himself, but no one sensed anything out of the ordinary about him. Then two days ago he doesn't show up for work. Phone calls went unanswered and finally they brought in the police to check on him at his address as they wondered if something bad had happened. Turns out he'd split. Paid up his bill where he was renting a flat and cleared out."

"So, he disappears right before Serafina is killed."

Slash nodded. "They gave me his employment identification number, but I have a feeling it and the name Alex Rogolli will lead nowhere. However, since they confirmed, via the photo you printed, that this is indeed the man who worked here, I have a better idea."

It took me about two nanoseconds to guess his train of thought. "Face recognition software?"

"*Si.* The pupil gets an A." He put an arm around

me. “I can access numerous databases and do a cross-reference. If he has a passport or a driver’s license, it shouldn’t us take too long to find our man.”

“Italian?”

He smiled. “It doesn’t matter, *cara.* Whatever the nationality, I’ll find him.”

We started to walk down the street and Slash kept his arm around me.

“So, um, Slash, I was wondering… Am I your pupil?”

He squeezed my shoulder. “Would you prefer to play the teacher?”

“Are we playing?”

“Not yet.”

Tito snorted behind us and I gave him a puzzled look over my shoulder. He snorted again. “Ah, dear Lexi. I see why Nico adores you.”

Slash murmured something in Italian.

Tito just laughed harder. “All this fresh air and love. It makes me hungry.”

I looked at him in disbelief. “Seriously? You just ate a plate of gnocchi. Make that two plates, since you ate most of mine.”

Slash steered me to the right. “I know a little café where we can pick up something to eat and take it back to the hotel. Besides, I want to check on the encryption program and get started on finding the real identity of Alex Rogolli.”

The café had cute little outdoor tables and umbrellas, though eating there would be like having lunch in the middle of a parking lot since people in Italy apparently thought it was okay to park your car on the sidewalk. As a result, I didn’t feel too disappointed about having lunch back in the hotel in front of a computer. Since I didn't have a clue what anything on the menu meant, Slash and Tito ordered. While we waited, I wandered out by the mostly-empty tables and watched as an elderly gentleman using an umbrella as a cane shuffled toward the cafe. Twice he almost tripped on the cobblestones and I debated whether I should go and help him or not. I didn't want him to fall, but on the other hand, I didn't want to insult him either.

He stumbled again, wavering on his feet and swinging his umbrella.

"Oh, for crying out loud." I scooted around a table and moved toward him.

I got about two steps away when Slash yelled something. I turned around just in time to see him flying through the air and crash directly into me and, by the force of gravity, the old man as well. My breath left my lungs with a sickening whoosh as I smashed into a table and my right knee and hip slammed against the cobblestones. I could hear shouting and screaming as people grappled on top of me and I tried to push them off.

At some point I managed to scramble away, just in time to see Slash roll to his feet and Tito take off down the street after a suddenly-turned-spry old man. People ran up to us saying things I didn't understand in Italian while Slash pulled me to my feet, patting me down like an airport security guard.

"What's going on?" My shoulder, arm and hip hurt and I saw my lunch all over the cobblestones.

"You okay, *cara?*"

"Of course, I'm not okay. I'm not having a very good day, if you haven't noticed." Not to mention the dead body, which I didn't point out, seeing as how we'd gathered a small crowd.

He pulled me to his chest. "Thank God, you're okay."

I looked down at my torn jeans, dirtied top and scraped elbow and hands. "This is your definition of okay? Why in the heck did you tackle me?"

Kneeling down beside the old man's umbrella, Slash picked it up gingerly, holding it in his hands.

"Slash? Who was that old guy? Where's Tito?"

Still examining the umbrella, Slash said something to the crowd and then hustled me away. "That old guy wasn't old. He tried to shoot you. Tito went after him."

I stopped in my tracks. "What? He tried to shoot me? Have you gone bonkers? I didn't see a gun."

"There was no gun." He held up the umbrella. "He tried to shoot you with this."

I stared at it in fascinated horror. "He tried to shoot me with a freaking umbrella?"

He angled the tip toward me. "See that opening? There was a dart inside."

I peered down at the dark hole. "Is this some kind of joke?"

"No joke, *cara.* Whether the dart held poison or a sedative, I don't know."

"Poison?" I screeched. "Why would a complete stranger want to shoot *me* with poison? No, wait. Don't answer that. Tell me why would he want to shoot me at all?"

Slash looked over his shoulder. "Someone thinks you're getting too close to something."

I stopped cold, looked into Slash's eyes. "Me?"

"*Si*, you, *cara*."

"How did you know? He was just an old man, for God's sake."

Slash brushed a fingertip across my cheek. "It's my job to know these things, *cara.* It was the way he held the umbrella, the manner in which he approached you, the look in his eyes. All of those things."

I shuddered. "To think I was trying to help him."

"*Si.* He expected that. But you're alive."

"Because of you."

"As soon as I get you safe, I'm going to go back and scour the area to try and find the dart. For the time being, I want you off the streets."

He pulled me into to his side so close that I kept stepping on his feet as we half-walked, half-ran toward the hotel.

"Jeez. Is this really necessary, Slash?"

"Absolutely. I will not let anything happen to you."

I didn't say another word until we got to the hotel. He didn't release me until we were at the room door.

"Stay back," he murmured, pulling a gun from out beneath his jacket. He checked the gadget on the doorjamb and murmured something under his breath. He slid open a little panel on it and pressed something until the light blinked green. Then he popped the gadget off and put it into his pocket. Sliding the entrance key down the door pad, he pressed down the handle and disappeared. After a moment, he came back and motioned for me to come in, still holding the gun.

"Someone tried to access the room," he said, closing the door behind him and sliding the deadbolt across. "We're going to have to move."

I looked around and everything seemed completely normal. Well, as normal as can be, given this day had turned into a never-ending nightmare. I'd seen a murdered girl and barely avoided being shot by a poison dart. What else could possibly happen? No, wait. I didn't want to know.

"How can you be sure?"

"My traps were sprung."

Walking over to the computer cluster, he checked on the progress of the encryption program.

"No movement on the big file. It's not budging. But we've cracked the other two."

"Want me to take a look?"

"Not now. Go pack. We're getting out of here."

There was a knock at the door and I jumped.

Slash strode across the room, standing to the side of the doorway, removing his gun from his shoulder holster and holding it up. "Who is it?"

"Tito."

Slash did a quick check through the peephole, slid open the deadbolt and opened the door. He dragged Tito inside by the front of his shirt, slamming the door behind him. "Did you catch him?"

Tito shook his head. "He got away. Had someone waiting for him in a vehicle a couple of blocks away. Did get this, though." He held up a white wig. "Maybe we can get some DNA from it." He looked over at me. "You okay, Lexi?"

"I'm not shot, if that's what you mean."

Tito slumped into a chair. "We shouldn't have left you alone out there. Who would have thought they'd try something like that with the two of us about?"

The lines around Slash's mouth tightened. "It was my mistake. It won't happen again. We're packing up."

"Where are you going?"

"Sperlonga."

I glanced over at Slash, who sat down in front of the terminals, shutting everything down. "What's Sperlonga?"

Tito answered for him. "You mean where. It's a town south of here on the coast. Nico is from Sperlonga."

"What about the police? I'm supposed to talk to them about Serafina."

"We'll stop by the station before we leave," Slash said, crawling under the table and unplugging cords. "Go pack, *cara.*"

Sighing, I went into my room and pulled out my suitcase, stuffing everything back inside. I hadn't even had time to enjoy the spectacular suite. When I came back, pulling my suitcase, Slash had almost packed up all the computer equipment. Tito was nowhere in sight.

"Need help?"

"Almost done." He stood, brushed off his jeans and walked up to me. "I don't like this turn of events." He took me by both of the shoulders, his expression serious. "I'm thinking about sending you back to Washington."

"What? No. *No.*"

His eyes darkened. "It's getting too dangerous."

"So you think I'm a sissy? I'm up to my neck in this now."

"I can do it without your permission. Terminate my contract with X-Corp."

"Don't threaten me. I'm not going to be shoved aside because you think I can't handle it. You need me and you know it."

He sighed, brushing my hair lightly with his hand. "Someone shot at you, *cara*. My heart stopped beating when I thought I might not reach you in time."

His confession touched me. "Really?"

"Really."

I tried to lighten the moment. "Look, it's not like I haven't been shot at before. Well, actually, I haven't ever been the target of a poison umbrella, but that's not the point…pun intended. I'm not running back to X-Corp because things got hot."

"Someone targeted you specifically, *cara.* That alone is alarming. But it's the method that worries me. These kinds of weapons are usually reserved for special branches of the government or high-powered private firms that can afford them. The fact that they used one of these in their attack against you is significant."

"In what way?"

"In the way that it signals to me they weren't trying to kill you, but kidnap you."

"Kidnap me?"

"They may suspect you've found something."

"The gateway program?"

"Not that, *cara.* Something else. You were the only one who had a firsthand look at Serafina's computer and enough time to copy some files, which is exactly what you did."

"Okay, but what's the significance? The police will now have access to those same files. It's not a big secret anymore."

Slash sighed. "Those police experts weren't even able to determine that Serafina was the inside link. You, however, took just a few hours to trace the hack. They aren't worried about the police discovering their secret, *cara.* They're worried *you* will."

I paused for a moment to think about it. "Okay, then why not just kill me? Not that I'm advocating that particular line of action, mind you. But why use an umbrella?"

"Why, indeed? Which leads me to the supposition I mentioned earlier that they don't want to harm you. At least not, yet. They either need to be certain what you know or…"

My pulse skipped a beat. "Or what?"

"Or they need to use your brainpower for another purpose, thus the kidnap attempt."

The light bulb flashed on. "The encrypted file. You think that file contains something they're worried about us finding."

"*Si*. I believe there's something unusual about that file. It's so far resisted every form of encryption-breaking program we've thrown at it and we've given it some pretty good ones. We're going to have to refine our approach."

"Even more reason for me to stay."

"Excuse me?"

"You need me, Slash. It'll take both of us to crack that file and you know it. I'm not going back to Washington with my tail tucked between my legs."

"You can't help me if you're harmed or missing."

"There's no guarantee I'll be safe back in Washington either. If I'm here, at the very least, you'll be able to keep an eye on me."

He frowned. "I will not let anyone harm you. Ever."

"Which is exactly why I'll be safe with you."

He searched my eyes for a moment and then abruptly released his hold on my shoulders. He strode to the window, yanking aside the drapes and staring out the window, leaning a forearm against the sill. At that moment it hit me how tired we both were—still jet-lagged, hungry and running on little more than adrenaline.

"There's something else, isn't there?" I took a step closer to him. "What aren't you telling me?"

For a minute neither of us spoke and then Slash sighed. "Tito went to see if he could retrieve the dart the man shot at you."

"Guess it doesn't really matter what he finds at this point."

"Not true. Whatever the substance inside, we might be able to trace it back to the manufacturer."

"Okay, but that's not all. What else?"

He exhaled a deep breath. "I think Serafina is the only person they had inside the bank, meaning the actual premises were physically impenetrable to them."

"So what? They didn't need actual access. They could do everything remotely. Heck, they could have wiped the drive if they wanted to."

"I know. So why didn't they?"

I pondered that a moment. "Good question. Do you think Serafina's death might have been unplanned?"

He shrugged. "Who knows? It's impossible to say how complicit she was in the entire process. Technically, all they needed her to do was open a program once she was inside the system."

"You think she was duped?"

"Perhaps. However, we also have to entertain the possibility that she knew full well what she was doing and held out for more money. There is also the chance she stumbled across her boyfriend's duplicity, if he's indeed a factor, and confronted him or decided to tell the authorities what she'd done because her conscience bothered her. It's difficult to say at this point."

I digested that thought. "Okay, but at some point, despite the apparent snail's pace of the police's tech force, it's fair to assume the hackers would realize the trail would eventually be traced back to her. But I checked, Slash. The gateway program wasn't malicious or self-destructive, which is weird because any decent hacker would have planted one just in case. Whoever wrote that program and then subsequently hid the trail was ace—way beyond decent. So, you're right, which leads us to the thousand-dollar question: why *didn't* the program have a self-destruct capability?"

Slash remained silent and the answer hit me like a ton of bricks. I felt stupid for not realizing it earlier.

"It's not just the money they're after."

"That's a distinct possibility."

"The encrypted file—the big one. You think whatever they want is in that file. But why didn't they just take the file, if they had remote access to her computer, and then destroy the original?"

"Excellent question." Slash rubbed the back of his neck. "That's what's bothering me. It doesn't make sense. It's not logical."

I smacked myself on the forehead. "Oh, jeez, Slash. Crap, crap, crap. I'm such a doofus. I know exactly why they didn't take the file. Her computer. Serafina shut her computer down. I had to boot it up. She denied them access. They must not have been able to access the computer remotely to get the file."

His eyes flashed in surprise. "Interesting. That definitely implies she was not cooperating with them."

My excitement grew. "I bet if we checked the date she obtained that file, it would be shortly before she shut down. But first, she hid it. Strictly amateur. They could have easily found the file if they knew she had it, but maybe they didn't know. We've got to crack it open, Slash."

"*Si.* I believe that what we have going on here is more than just the siphoning of Vatican funds. It's something else. Something big."

I walked over to Slash, put my hand on his shoulder. "If whoever killed Serafina has any contacts inside the police force, they'll have that file by now."

"I know. But we have it, too, *cara.* That's what has

them running scared. Now the race is on to see who can open it first and discover what's inside. Apparently, they aren't getting anywhere and are worried that we are."

"Good. Does that mean I'm still on the team?"

He grabbed a fistful of my T-shirt and yanked me into his chest. "I don't really like this. I want you to understand that. But from this moment on, you're with me unless I say otherwise. You must do as I say, stay close to me, and no heroics of any kind. Understood?"

"Actually, I'm the least heroic person I know."

He narrowed his eyes. "You're not agreeing to anything, are you?"

"Not really."

"Ah, *cara.* What am I to do with you?"

He slid his hand behind the back of my neck and then lowered his head to kiss me. His lips were soft and tender.

All rational thought fled from my brain. When he pulled away, I nearly collapsed to the floor. All this kissing was seriously confusing me, not to mention making me hot in places better not discussed. I was pretty sure this kind of kissing, involving a hand behind my neck and focused tenderness on my lips, did not occur between people who were just casual friends. Still, I didn't know exactly what it meant to Slash. I needed my best friend and social director, Basia, to help me figure it all out, but she was a continent away and I was about to go on the lam alone with Slash. I couldn't see how that would clarify matters any.

Still, if I looked at the bright side, I remained on the team. Unfortunately, I had a heck of a lot to be worried about. Only the part that scared me the most didn't involve computers, encrypted files and poison umbrellas. Just elegant hacker hands and one heck of a good kiss.

Chapter Six

Slash took a few minutes to pack his personal items. Tito returned just as we were heading out.

He held up a clear plastic bag and inside was a small dart. I shivered looking at it, knowing it had been aimed at me and wondering what was in it.

Slash took the bag and tucked it into a side pocket on his black duffel. "Good work, Tito."

Tito nodded. "I'm going to see if I can take a few days off. Meet you down in Sperlonga. You might be able to use my help."

"Be careful, my friend. You may have been identified."

Tito put his hand on the door handle. "Will do. See you soon." He pointed a finger at me. "You be careful of old men."

"No kidding. It's at the top on my list."

He left and Slash followed him out to get a bellhop cart to lug our stuff downstairs. We checked out of the hotel and the valet pulled Slash's sedan around. Slash made me sit safely in the car while he packed everything in the trunk.

The trip to the police station went smoother than expected, at least for the time being. My nerves were jangling as I showed my passport and explained how, on behalf of X-Corp, I had traced the hack to Serafina's computer. I volunteered no technical information on how I discovered the hack, next to nothing about my look on her computer, and absolutely zip on the trip to her apartment where I discovered her dead body. I was relieved I didn't have to lie outright, but it still made me nervous as heck that at some point down the line, I could be charged with what could technically be considered illegal omission. Finding a dead body and then not mentioning it during a police investigation would *not* be considered a good thing. However, the detective seemed satisfied for the time being with my answers. Thankfully I wasn't a suspect in any way. They were just seeking information.

I followed Slash out of the station. "Whew, that wasn't as bad as I expected. How'd I do?"

"Excellent."

"Well, I'm surprised he didn't insist on me staying in town."

"He did."

I stopped. "What? Did you tell him we were leaving?"

He shrugged. "If he needs to speak with you, *cara*, he can. He has my number."

I suppressed the urge to hyperventilate, trying not to stress over whether I'd make it out of Italy without a lengthy stint in jail. We climbed back in the car and Slash drove through the city at a breathtaking speed, weaving in and out of traffic without a moment's hesitation or fear. I closed my eyes and tried to think in a positive manner. After all, if I died in a car accident, I wouldn't have to worry about umbrella darts or jail time.

I don't know how long I kept my eyes closed, but

when I woke up we were well out of the city and I could see the coast from the window.

"Jeez, I fell asleep?" I squiggled in my seat and tried to stretch a cramp out of my left calf.

He slid his hand off the gearshift and over to my knee, patting it. My pulse spiked. Why was I so jumpy around him?

I shook my head trying to clear it. Maybe I was more tired than I thought. But holy cow, did he have to look so good with his tousled black hair and a sexy five-o'clock shadow that gave him an even more dangerous air than he already had? Not to mention that he'd left his hand where it was on my knee and it was burning a hole through my jeans.

I gave myself a mental slap, reminding myself to stay on task. "Focus, Carmichael."

Slash turned his head. "Did you say something?"

"No. Yes. Never mind. Where are we?"

"Minutes from home."

I looked back out the window and saw a gorgeous stretch of white beach surrounded by rocky cliffs. A structure of some kind had been built into the rock.

I sat up in my seat, staring at the sight with an open mouth. "That's stunning."

Slash smiled. "It's Tiberius's Villa. Well, what's left of it, anyway."

"Tiberius as in the Roman emperor?"

"*Si*. If we have time, I'll show you his grotto. It's spectacular and remarkably well preserved."

He drove into the charming town and through a few winding side streets. There was a beach view from almost every angle and it was breathtaking.

Slash opened his window and took a deep breath. I could smell the salt from the ocean. "Tourism is our main attraction here. Most people come for the beaches, but the historical sites are a big draw as well."

"You're lucky to have grown up here. It's beyond beautiful. Does all your family live in Sperlonga?"

"Not any more. Just Nonna and a handful of my cousins. My mother and stepfather live in Naples. Stefano lives in London and Giorgio is in Florence."

"No sisters?"

"No sisters."

After a minute, he pulled into a small driveway in front of a yellow house. The yard was immaculate and well landscaped. We climbed out of the car and he came around to take my hand. Together we went to the front door. Instead of knocking, he simply opened the door and stepped in.

"Nonna?"

An elderly lady with silver hair in a bun stepped into sight. She saw Slash and her entire face lit up.

"*Chierichetto!*" she called out to him, cupping his cheeks between her hands and kissing both cheeks. He enveloped her in a big bear hug and she squealed with delight. I couldn't help but smile.

He pulled away, saying something to her in Italian. She turned her gaze on me, her bright blue eyes seeming to pin me to the spot with laser intensity.

Swallowing my sudden nervousness, I held out a hand. "Uh, hi."

Her lips turned up into a smile and she put her hand in mine. Although small, she squeezed with the strength of a linebacker and I had to swallow my wince.

She said something else and Slash put his arm around each of us, ushering us further into the house. "She's going to fix us something to eat. Now, *cara*, you will taste true Italian cooking."

Frankly, I was starving, so I would have eaten anything, including the kitchen sink. But the prospect of having real Italian food made my stomach gurgle so loudly that both Slash and his grandmother looked at me. I grinned and lifted my shoulders in a sheepish shrug.

Slash pointed me to a kitchen chair. "Sit. I'll unload the car."

I grabbed his arm. There was no way on God's green earth I was going to be left alone with his grandmother. What if something happened? What if she took a swing at me or I insulted her by accident? It was painfully clear I needed constant supervision when interacting with his acquaintances, especially Italian ones.

"I'll help. Really."

I knew my voice bordered on desperation. But Slash just smiled. He probably knew what was going through my mind.

"Okay, *cara*. Come on."

He said something to his grandmother and she kissed him again as if she couldn't believe he had come to visit. We unloaded the car and piled all our computer equipment in a small sewing room with a long table and a flowered couch. Slash put the sewing machine in a corner of the room and we began to set up on the table. Once we'd finished, we headed back down to the kitchen where Nonna was cooking something that had a delicious aroma.

I lifted my nose in the air. "Oh, my God. Whatever that is, it smells like heaven."

Slash put his hand in the small of my back, ushering me into the kitchen. He parked me at the kitchen table with a glass of Italian red wine while he stood at the counter and helped Nonna cook. I couldn't help but watch in fascination as he expertly chopped, diced and sliced vegetables with laser precision, all the while sipping wine and carrying on a lively conversation with his grandmother. A couple of times I almost had a heart attack as Nonna said something to him and gestured wildly, a knife still in her hand. Slash didn't miss a beat or even duck, acting as if it was completely normal. All this hand gesturing and kissing was apparently an intuitive part of being Italian. I was fascinated by it even if I didn't get it.

After some time had passed, I began to feel useless just sitting there. Against my better judgment, I offered to help.

Slash raised a dark eyebrow. Nonna said something and Slash smiled.

"Nonna wants to know if you have a particular cooking specialty."

Sure, I knew what my specialty was—cornflakes. But I had to say something. "Um, corn. And corn derivatives."

Slash's smile widened. He knew me better than I thought. I had to tread cautiously here.

He crooked a finger at me. "Come here, *cara*. You can help me chop."

I was a danger to myself, Slash, and possibly all of Italian society with a knife, but I put on a brave face. "Okay. I'd better wash up first. Where's the bathroom?"

Slash pointed behind me and I headed in that direction. The bathroom was tiny and held not only a sink and a toilet, but a small washing machine as well. No dryer, I guess. A laundry line had been strung across the room and I had to duck beneath underwear, bras and panty hose to get to the toilet.

I went to the bathroom and was about to wash my

hands when I heard something beneath the sink. I bent down and nearly jumped out of my skin as a large gray cat with green eyes peered out at me.

"Jeez." I didn't know when I'd become so jumpy. I guess dead bodies and shooting umbrellas can be unnerving. I pressed my hand against my chest to calm my heart. "Okay. Thank goodness, I didn't have a heart attack."

I knelt and held out a hand. "Hi, kitty. What's your name?"

The cat arched its back and hissed at me. I quickly drew my hand back. "Okay, I get it. I'm the intruder here. Don't let me keep you from your business." I waved a hand at the kitty litter box. "Go for it."

To my surprise, the cat walked around in a circle and then peed on the floor in front of the toilet. I stared at the puddle on the floor. I'd never had a cat before. Actually I'd never owned *any* kind of pet before, so I wasn't sure what to make of this. I washed my hands and then opened the door to the bathroom. The cat streaked out. I returned to the kitchen and saw Slash was missing.

Nonna pointed upstairs and I nodded.

"Okay. Um, your cat. She peed on the floor."

Nonna shook her head. She didn't have a clue what I was saying. I tried to demonstrate, but realized it was awkward pretending I was peeing. I tried meowing, but I still wasn't getting anywhere.

Thankfully, Slash returned to the kitchen as I was circling around the kitchen acting like a cat and pretending to pee. He stared at me in amazement.

"I'm trying to tell your grandmother that the cat just peed on the floor in the bathroom."

"*What?*"

"The cat. She left a puddle on the floor in the bathroom. I didn't know how I should clean it up."

Slashed stared at me for a long moment. "*Cara*, cats don't pee on the floor. They aren't dogs. They have litter boxes."

"Tell me about it. You can see why I'm so shocked."

Slash said something to his grandmother and she replied angrily.

"She says Principessa has never peed on the floor in her life."

"Principessa?"

"The cat."

"Oh, right. Well, I swear, she did it right in front of me—on the floor by the toilet."

Slash said something to Nonna and she took off for the bathroom, screeching.

I lifted my hands. "I swear I didn't even touch it."

Nonna came back to the kitchen with the large gray cat in her arms. It stared at me with big green eyes, its tail swishing.

Nonna murmured, while stroking it. "Principessa."

"Is the cat okay?"

"Nonna thinks you might have scared her."

"Me? She was hiding under the sink. I freaked out when I saw her. I wasn't expecting a cat in the bathroom. Oh, jeez. Now she thinks I terrorize cats."

Slash put a hand on my shoulder. "It's okay. I'll go clean it up."

Slash disappeared. Nonna sat with the cat that kept staring at me as if I was the devil incarnate. I swallowed my entire glass of wine in a few gulps.

Slash returned a few minutes later. "All clean. Now, *cara*, I do believe you were about ready to show us your superior skills in the kitchen."

After the cat incident, I needed a carafe of wine to persuade me to help. "Um, well, about that."

"Didn't you offer to help?"

"Yes. But… Nonna isn't making corn."

"Or cornflakes."

"Hey, have you been snooping in my cupboards?"

"Ah, contraire. I'm quite observant. You don't put them in your cupboard, *cara.* The box has a permanent spot on your counter."

He had me there.

He smiled, picked up my wineglass and filled it again. "I'm teasing you. Dinner is already finished. Come on, let's eat."

Nonna set Principessa down and Slash began carrying dishes to the kitchen table. I helped set the forks, knives, and napkins while Nonna put the finishing touches on the food.

We sat and Nonna brought over a large covered dish. She took off the lid and I forgot all about the cat. "Is that…lasagna?"

Slash smiled. "No. That's not lasagna. That's Nonna's lasagna."

I could not believe the amazing smell that came from the dish. She served up Slash and I large servings, giving herself a piece about one-fourth the size of ours. Before we ate, she said a prayer in Italian. I folded my hands in my lap, but I peeked and saw Slash had closed his eyes and was murmuring the words with her.

I didn't waste any time digging in. Slash pulled off a piece of bread from a loaf of thick, crusted bread and handed it to me, while Nonna plied me with a vegetable dish called *fenoci in salata.* I must have died and gone to food heaven.

I had two helpings of the lasagna, two pieces of

bread, an extra helping of the salad and another glass of wine. It took us an inordinately long time to eat, but I'm certain it would stand as one of the most memorable meals of all time. I was so busy eating I didn't even have time to talk much. Nonna didn't speak English, and it made for a darn near perfect dinner situation for me.

During dinner Slash laughed and smiled. I'd never seen him more relaxed and happy. He was truly in his element and I could see how fond he was of his grandmother. After my third glass of wine, I actually became rather chatty. I must have thanked her a dozen times for such an incredible meal. It was better than any restaurant I'd ever been to and probably would ever visit in my entire life. I don't think I'd ever been so happily stuffed.

I helped clear the table, but Nonna wouldn't let either Slash or I assist her with the dishes.

Slash put a companionable arm around my shoulders. "She told us to get out of her kitchen and go play with our hi-tech toys so we can save Uncle Benedetto's skin."

"Really?"

"Really."

"I'm in love with your grandmother. Although I'm pretty sure I just gained thirty pounds from that meal."

"Every meal is like that at Nonna's."

"How is it she's so thin?"

"She expends a lot of energy cooking."

"Ah, the physics of exertion."

"Exactly. You made her happy by eating so much."

"Well, I'm pretty sure my stomach has never been happier. So, there you have it. Two peas in a pod."

We started to walk toward the stairs. I'm glad Slash still had his arm around me because I felt a little tipsy. "Hey, what did she call you when we first arrived? It was cheery something."

"*Chierichetto.*"

"Yes, that's it. What does it mean?"

"Altar boy."

I stopped. "You were an altar boy?"

"That surprises you?" He grinned, reached beneath his sweater and pulled out his gold cross. He kissed it once and then tucked it back inside.

That was Slash for you. Mystery and enigma all rolled into one. Master hacker, secret agent, a former or current employee of a Vatican secret service that didn't officially exist, a hot male specimen, *and* an altar boy. I wasn't sure I'd ever figure him out.

But I sure did enjoy a good challenge.

Chapter Seven

I grabbed the banister and wobbled onto the first step. "I take it that your given name is not *chierichetto.*"

Slash laughed as we climbed the stairs. "*Cara*, you can call me whatever you'd like. Just as long as you call me."

I groaned. "Ha, ha."

We entered the sewing room and Slash sat down in a chair facing one of the laptops. I realized we'd taken a long break from hacking and that I was looking forward to taking another crack at that big encrypted file. I would certainly be more relaxed and energized now. It occurred to me that Slash had known that all along and I felt a rush of gratitude toward him.

Slash glanced over at me and caught me staring. Could I act any more like a socially clueless teenager?

"Shall we see what's in those two encrypted files we cracked, *cara?*"

"Sure. I thought you'd never ask." I stood behind him and leaned over his shoulder as he opened the first file. "What is it?"

He scanned the document. "Financial statements. Payments, I think."

"For what and to whom?"

"I'm not sure. I'll have to study it in greater detail. Let's take a quick look at the other file."

He clicked it open. "That's strange."

"What's strange?"

Slash rubbed his unshaven chin as he read. "It's a news article from a local paper."

"About what?"

He read a bit more. "The Vatican archives." He sighed. "I was hoping for something a lot more substantial in such a heavily encrypted file. This is public knowledge."

"Maybe there's something else in there. Or it has some kind of special significance."

"Perhaps. I'll read it carefully. But which file to deal with first? The spreadsheet or the news article?"

I sat in the chair next to him. "Actually, Slash, I've been meaning to talk to you about something. It's the hack."

He turned his full attention on me, those mysterious brown eyes regarding me thoughtfully. "What are you thinking, *cara?*"

"Well, I just don't get it. Why do you think they targeted the Vatican Bank in the first place?"

"Money?"

"Yes, but that doesn't feel like the whole story here. Despite the fact that money was stolen, it doesn't seem like a simple hack and grab to me. With hacking skills this good, these guys could have got into another, *way* less visible, bank much easier and with a thousand times less the risk. So, is it religion? Politics? And if so, where's the message, the public statement?"

Slash nodded, his eyes thoughtful. "*Si*. Good point. We've been so busy tracing the hack, dealing with the fallout, we haven't taken time to think about the why."

"Exactly. I'm also not getting the vibe that it was a hack to show-off because technically they didn't hack in—they were *let* in. Any decent hacker knows that's a big difference."

I pulled my hair into a ponytail, but I didn't have a band, so it fell loose again. "It's just that the hack…it felt almost as if it were *designed* to be flashy. Someone purposefully wanted the hack to be discovered quickly, but made the trail so hard that unraveling it would take significant time."

"*Si*, but why?"

"I don't know." I leaned back in the chair, closed my eyes. I needed to think like a hacker. What would be my motivations for such a strange series of actions? Why would I commit a high-profile hack, sure to be noticed, but at the same time want to ensure it couldn't be traced…at least not quickly? It didn't make sense. Why in the world would I design a hack intended to get a lot of attention, if I really didn't want anyone to trace me? It was crazy.

Unless…

I jumped up from the couch. "That's it. It has to be it."

"What's it?"

"It's got to be a diversion, Slash. The real target is somewhere else. They want everyone busy on the hack at the Vatican Bank—"

"—so they can hack elsewhere in peace. Brilliant, *cara*."

"No, no. Not so brilliant. Not yet. It still doesn't answer the question of *why* the Vatican Bank and *where* they intend to hack. There has to be a connection."

Slash snapped his fingers. "The archives."

"As in Vatican archives? Great idea, except you can't hack into something that isn't digital."

"That's the point." Slash leaned forward, his eyes gleaming. "For the past ten years, the Vatican has been quietly and methodically going through the archives, cataloguing, photographing, and converting priceless documents, paintings and other historically significant items, into digital files."

"Once the material is digital, it becomes vulnerable." I considered for a moment. "This could be big."

"Bigger than we imagined."

I inhaled a breath, my brain humming. "Okay. Now we are starting to make sense. It's possible the hack at the Vatican bank is intended to keep the police preoccupied so they can hack unnoticed into the new digital files of the Vatican archives with little to no detection."

"*Si*, but there's one problem."

"Which is?"

"You. They didn't count on you, *cara*. They expected the trace to take significantly more time. You didn't give it to them."

"Which means?"

Slash turned in his chair and studied the monitor. "I'm not sure. Not yet. But I have my suspicions."

"No fair. Share."

"I will, *cara*. I promise. Just give me a minute to read this article. I need a moment to get my thoughts together."

I stood and started pacing while he read the article. Then he flipped over to the financial statements and scrolled down through the file. After a moment, he rose from his chair and examined the big encrypted file on which we were making exactly zip progress. He leaned over, started another protocol on the file and straight-

ened. He rolled his shoulders a couple of times and sat down on the couch, patting the cushion beside him.

"Okay, come here. I have a theory."

I plopped down on the couch next to him. "Spill."

"There is something unusual about that big file. The file we are not able to crack."

"It does seem to contain a strange form of encryption. Nothing seems to be working."

"I may know where it originated."

"You do?"

"Potentially. I've heard of a group who have been working on a new protocol utilizing some newer aspects of deniable encryption."

I straightened. My interest was piqued to say the least. Deniable encryption was cool stuff. It permitted users to deny the very existence of specific encrypted data. I was well versed in its theoretical aspects, but I hadn't seen it in action.

"Okay. You've got my full attention. Where exactly is this group located? The NSA? The CIA?"

Slash exhaled a breath. "The Vatican."

I shouldn't have been surprised, but I was. It's just I didn't naturally connect sophisticated hackers and priests in the same sentence. Then I thought about Slash and his background and I remained silent, waiting for him to continue.

He leaned forward, resting his elbows on his knees. "I considered the possibility of an advanced form of deniable encryption with some unusual twists when I first saw the file, but I quickly discarded the possibility as too conjectural. I hadn't heard of a practical application yet occurring."

"But you're considering it now."

"*Si*. I just started a new protocol designed to see if

we can make any headway. But the truth is, *cara*, if that file what I think it is, we are facing big trouble."

"Why? Do you think it's something from the Vatican's archives?"

"No. Not just the archives. The *secret* archives."

"There are secret archives? Really? Why?"

A faint smile touched his lips. "There are some things so sacred and personal to the Holy Order they are not for public consumption."

That didn't make a whole lot of sense to me, but my religious knowledge was shaky, so I didn't ask for clarification.

"Okay, so that news article we just cracked, did it refer to these secret archives?"

"No. But I've got a feeling."

I trusted his feelings completely. "Okay, so then who put that news article on Serafina's hard drive?"

Slash rubbed his chin. "Perhaps Serafina herself. It looks like someone pulled it up off a local newspaper website just a few days ago."

"If it were her, there was no way she encrypted it herself."

"No. But perhaps she suspected something was up. Overheard a conversation or something. She wanted more information."

I considered. "It's plausible. Maybe one of the hackers saw it—saw what she was reading and got nervous. Perhaps even Marcus, Alex, or whatever his real name is, himself. He figured she knew. So, he encrypted the file and protected it from any casual onlookers. He probably meant to go back and delete it later. But he confronted her first."

Slash nodded. "It fits. Maybe she spilled her suspicions to him. Or maybe he made her talk."

I shuddered, remembering how she looked lying in the bed with a slit throat. "Still, she wasn't dumb. She shut down her computer before she met with him. Smart girl. He didn't expect that. He couldn't get in again."

"*Si*. He had no time to clean house. Then we came."

"Okay. So, in the big picture, what does it mean in terms of this freakishly hard-to-crack file? And why did Serafina have it on her hard drive?"

Slash spread his hands. "Easy. They hacked into the secret archives via her account."

I nodded, my thoughts whirling. "Yes, yes. That makes sense. They'd have fewer barriers hacking from within a Vatican institution. They just didn't have time to either extract it completely or delete the file from her hard drive before Serafina shut down her computer, locking them out."

"That is the most likely scenario."

I pressed my hand against my forehead. "Then this is really looking like Serafina was not cooperating. I think she discovered she'd been duped."

"I'm afraid so, *cara*."

I hopped up from the couch and started pacing again. "Then we are too late."

"No. I don't think so.

I raised an eyebrow. "Why not? They have the file just as we do."

"They may have the file, but I would presume they haven't been able to crack the encryption yet either. We've had the about same amount of time and while they may be good, we're better. I think they knew this well before we did, which is why they tried to kidnap you."

"The solution is easy, right? Can't you just talk to

the people at the Vatican archives who encrypted this file? Ask them for the key? You're one of them, right?"

"It's not so simple. Technically I work for the U.S. government, *cara*. I no longer have the same rights, access, or privileges at the Vatican as I once did. Of course, I have connections and I will exploit them, but it will take time. Time I'm afraid we don't have."

I glanced over at the computer running the new encryption protocol. "What the *heck* is in that file?"

"I don't know, *cara*. But one person has already died for it."

I sat down in front of one of the other laptops. "I'm going to read up on deniable encryption."

He sat next to me. "Good idea."

I slid on my glasses and pulled up some technical information. I was surprised at the speed of the connection in coastal Italy. "Your grandmother has a good wireless service."

"Nothing but the best for my girls. You should see her alarm system."

He brushed my hair back from my shoulder, ran his fingers along the side of my neck. "I'm going to start running the face recognition program on Alex Rogolli." I thought he might say something else, but he cleared his throat and turned away.

I started to read, but the big meal and wine had made me impossibly sleepy and the words began to run together. Even worse, Nonna brought us dessert—tea, cookies and sweets. I couldn't stop shoveling it all in my mouth. I wondered if she hadn't put something addicting in the food that kept my hand moving methodically from the plate to my mouth. Jeez, it was a wonder that with food like this all Italians didn't weigh a million pounds.

Feeling like a slouch because at least I'd had a nap in the car and he hadn't, I tried to plug on, but after about an hour, I couldn't keep my eyes open and couldn't even remember if I'd read one interesting thing.

Slash must have noticed my head nearly banging the keyboard because, at some point, he came up behind me. "Off to bed, *cara*." He eased me out of the chair and propelled me toward the doorway.

I mumbled with eyes half-mast. "No, no. I'm good. Really. I just need a minute. I'll just crash here on the couch."

I pulled out of his grip and wobbled toward the flowered couch where I collapsed. "Just a minute or two, 'kay?"

Sighing, Slash knelt beside the couch, lifting my arm and tucking a quilt over me. It smelled like roses and lavender. On the other hand, Slash smelled like pasta, red wine and sexy man.

I yawned. "Why aren't you tired? I had a nap and I still can't keep my eyes open."

"It's Nonna's cooking. It's hard to do anything after one of her meals."

"She's an amazing cook. I may ask her to marry me."

He grinned. "You won't have been the first. I'm going to run an analysis on a few more things and then I'm out as well." He placed a soft kiss on my forehead. "*Buona notte, cara.*"

Without really thinking about what I was doing, I took his chin in my hand, raised my mouth to his and kissed him back. See, I could do the Italian thing, too.

He tasted like wine and his mouth was hot and soft. "Hmmmm. Good night, Slash."

I closed my eyes, but I didn't feel him leaving, so I peeked them open again. He was staring at me.

Uh, oh, I thought, all vestiges of sleepiness vaporizing in an instant. He looked at me with a fierce, almost predatory look. My cheeks heated and I started to apologize when he leaned down and kissed me, again, effectively shutting me up. His lips scorched mine and I forgot everything except the exquisite feel of his mouth. After a few moments, he lifted his lips, but his mouth lingered against the corner of my mouth.

"Do you know what you're doing, *cara?*" he murmured. "Playing with fire."

My heart pounded and all I could think about was how much I wished he'd just stop talking and kiss me again. But he deserved an explanation of my temporary insanity.

I wiggled until he lifted his head. "I'm sorry, Slash. I'm an idiot. The wine and jet-lag has impaired my thinking. I'm not sure why I kissed you like that…on the mouth. I thought while in Rome, I should do as the Romans do. However, it's painfully obvious that I've not mastered the social appropriateness of when or to whom or where to offer such a kiss."

For a moment he just gazed at me and then he laughed softly. That was the second time in so many days he'd laughed openly at me. Indignant, I tried to sit up just as he bent down. My forehead smashed into his nose.

Slash cursed and pressed his hand to his nose.

I looked at him in horror. "Oh, my God. I'm so sorry. It's just you were laughing at me—"

I tried to sit up, but lost my balance. I fell into him, my hands against his chest, almost as if I were pushing him backward. He tried to steady me, but one hand was on his nose and he lost his balance, too. We ended up falling to the floor with Slash pulling me on top of him. That's when I looked to my right and saw the tips of a pair of beige patent shoes.

Slash must have seen them too, because we both instantly stilled.

"*Per amor di Dio!*"

Horrified, I looked up to where Nonna stood glaring down at us. Slash rolled sideways and hopped to his feet, a chagrined look on his face. Thankfully, I didn't see any blood on his nose. Yet. There was still time for her to clock him one and me after that.

Without a word, Slash held out a hand and pulled me to my feet. He said something to his grandmother in Italian and she answered crisply before turning and marching away.

"Oh, God, oh, God, oh, God." I was hyperventilating. "That looked all wrong. I mean, if taken out of context, of course. Oh, jeez. Did I break your nose?"

"Not yet."

"Do you think Nonna got the wrong impression? Did you tell her I was just practicing Italian methods of showing affection? Well, except for the last part when I smashed your nose and fell to the floor on top of you." I didn't think it scientifically possible, but I had started hyperventilating and babbling at the same time. "What did she say?"

Slash gingerly touched the bridge of his nose. He didn't seem all that concerned about Nonna's untimely presence.

"Do you really want to know what Nonna said, *cara?*"

"Yes. No. Jeez, better to know I guess."

"Loosely translated…she told us to get a room already."

"*What*?" I hid my face in my hands. "Oh, no. No,

no, no. No more wine or excellent Italian food for me *ever* again."

Slash came over to me and took both of my hands in his. "You mastered the Italian way perfectly."

I lifted my face. "I did?"

He put a finger under my chin and nudged it up until I looked into his eyes. "Attraction and affection can be powerful emotions. Italians know that better than most. But you should be warned. You've now opened a door to me. I'll not back out so easily."

I stared at him. Holy freaking cow. I had no clue what *that* was supposed to signify. I made a mental note to call Basia as soon as I could. Of course, I'd have to call as soon as I wasn't under dire threat of being kidnapped, shot by a poison umbrella, or possibly going to prison for conveniently omitting the fact that I'd found a dead body. Now I had to add being murdered in my sleep by a disgruntled Italian grandma to the list.

Still, his words seemed significant. How was it that *I'd* opened the door? Had I ever kissed him before? Yes, plenty of times. But...but he'd always been the one kissing me first. Jeez, was this the first time I'd ever initiated a kiss with *him*? Did that mean something? Had I opened a door? To what?

Oh, God. I'd also better find out what it all of this meant in terms of my relationship, or non-relationship, with Finn. Right now I had too many unknown variables. Without variables or, at the very least, a working formula, I was at a complete loss.

What I did know was that I'd kissed Finn and now I'd kissed Slash. And I mean *kissed.* So, did that mean I had a relationship with both of them...or neither? Did this make me easy or just easily confused?

Slash tucked a strand of hair behind my ear. "Don't think so hard, *cara.* All will be well."

That made the second man in just a few days to tell me not to overthink the relationship thing. As I'm apparently missing the socially intuitive in chip, how else could I figure things out? Why the heck was it all so complicated?

I needed time to process. As a result, I went to where I felt safest. I took a seat in front of the laptop and examined the progress on the encrypted file. "We're getting exactly nowhere."

He sighed. "I know. Frankly, I'm too tired to think of how to approach it next."

"You didn't seem all that tired a minute ago."

He smiled. "Come here and I might just get a second wind."

I wisely stayed where I was and kept my mouth shut.

When Slash saw I wasn't returning, he stretched. "We're both worn out. Come on, *cara*, let's just go to bed."

My eyes widened and I turned in the chair. "Um… well…ah…"

He sighed. "In separate rooms."

I let out a breath of relief. Perhaps my face showed all my emotions because Slash took my hand and pulled me up and into his embrace. I laid my head against his chest and heard the steady thump of his heart. He stroked my hair with his hand.

"I'm going to amend that statement. You're not getting off that easy, *cara.*" He kissed the top of my head. "Tonight we sleep alone. But after that, I offer no promises."

Chapter Eight

Slash led me to a small but charming bedroom with a dresser and bed. My suitcase stood in one corner and there were fresh towels on the flowered bedspread. I undressed and crawled under the covers in my bra and panties, too tired to brush my teeth or even unpack my suitcase to find my pajamas. I could hear someone moving around in the room next to me and wondered if it were Slash or Nonna. I must not have pondered for too long because the next thing I knew sun streamed in through a part in the curtains and I was ravenously hungry again.

I got up, pulled on a bathrobe, and took some clean clothes out of the suitcase. Praying I wouldn't run into Nonna before I had a shower, I made my way down the hall to the small bathroom. Luckily it was empty. I took a quick, mostly cold shower in a clawed tub with a handheld nozzle and no shower curtain. The shower took ten minutes, but it took me another twenty to mop up the water I'd sprayed everywhere trying to wash my hair. The Italians were brilliant cooks and enviously friendly, but apparently they were clueless when it came to shower curtains.

I'd used every towel she'd given me, plus the two others already in the bathroom by the time I'd finished. I didn't want to judge, but it seemed counterproductive to have a showerhead if you didn't have a curtain. But given what happened last night, I didn't feel in any position to give Nonna housekeeping tips.

I dressed in clean jeans and a sweater before combing out my hair and hooking my computer glasses on the front of my shirt. I figured hacking would be the choice of action for the day.

I went downstairs to the kitchen. It was empty. I heard some voices outside, so I went to the door, pulled aside the white gauzy curtain and looked out. Slash was talking to a man by a red car. Slash passed him a plastic bag and I realized it was the one that held the dart that had almost got me.

I was standing by the counter when Slash came back in. He seemed startled to see me. "Good morning, *cara*. How did you sleep?"

"Like a log. Seems like I'm the last one up. Where's Nonna?"

"She went to the store." He pressed a kiss against my cheek, completely casual-like. "Did you have any dreams?"

My face heated. It sounded really sexy, the way he asked me that, and my body responded with a weird tingle. I shook my head. "Ah, I don't think so. So, how's your nose?"

"I don't have any black eyes."

"That's a good thing, right?"

He smiled, gave my hair a tug. "Ready for breakfast?"

I put my hands in my pockets. "Sure. Who was that outside?"

"A friend. He'll find out what's inside that dart."

"I guess that's good."

"We need to know." He picked up a plate of croissant-like pastries piled on a plate. "I'll bring the cornetti and you bring the coffee." He jerked his head toward an old-fashioned coffee machine. Two mugs were nearby and I poured the coffee in, adding at least half a cup of milk to mine.

We headed back up to the sewing room and sat down in front of the laptops. Slash took the one running the encryption and I took the laptop next to him.

I picked up one of the croissants and gingerly took a bite. "Oh, my God!" I stuffed the rest of the pastry in my mouth. "It's got chocolate." I chewed with my eyes closed to savor the moment. "Any nationality that permits eating chocolate for breakfast is number one in my book." Picking up a cloth napkin, I wiped the crumbs from my lips. "Have I mentioned I love Italy?"

He smiled. "You'd be surprised what we often have for breakfast, *cara*, and it's not always food."

"What is there other than food?"

He chuckled. "Ah, but I have a lot to teach you."

Jeez. There went that tingle again. It was like I had no control over my own body. Slash said something, provocative or not, and my body leapt to whatever conclusion it wanted. And right now, it wanted him.

I coughed and wiped my hands. "Okay, what's up?"

"I ran into a snag with the facial recognition software for Alex Rogolli. I'm running it again. If he's in the system, we should have the results shortly. I've sent the financial spreadsheet to Uncle Benedetto and asked for his thoughts on it. I've put out feelers to my contacts in the Vatican. We are working off suspicions here, so I have to be careful what I say."

"You've been a busy boy this morning." I looked over

at Slash's computer, the one running the encryption on the big file. "Any luck there?"

"A bit of progress. I think we're on the right path. Deniable encryption is where we need to focus."

"We've got to get into that file and fast."

He took a sip of his coffee. "Want a look since I've altered the protocol?"

Boy, did I ever. He stood and I took his chair, sliding my glasses onto my nose. I didn't know a lot about deniable encryption, but I was now familiar enough with the basics that I felt confident enough to play. At first I felt self-conscious with Slash standing behind me watching, but after a while I became so absorbed that I even didn't notice him sit down and slide the plate of cornetti toward me. I also didn't realize that I'd eaten the entire plate until I noticed the chocolate on the keyboard. Looking up in surprise, I blinked as Slash snapped his cell phone closed and handed me a napkin. Jeez, I'd been so intent I hadn't even heard him talking.

I slid the glasses off my nose and rubbed my eyes. "How long have I been at it?"

"Just over an hour."

"I've gone exactly nowhere."

"I noticed."

I took a sip of my stone cold coffee. "What in the world is in this file?"

"I would say something infinitely interesting. It's masterfully encrypted, but not impenetrable. We'll get in. Unfortunately, time is of the essence."

"So, what next?"

Slash leaned back in his chair. "I've got news on the dart. We know the substance was a sedative."

I wasn't sure if I should feel relieved or horrified. "So, no one was trying to kill me?"

"Not at that point. But the interesting thing is, it's an unusual sedative."

"What's unusual about it?"

"It has the typical elements of benzodiazepine, a sedative, but it also contained a significant amount of sodium thiopental and amobarbital."

I raised an eyebrow. "You're going to have to speak English. I left my medical degree in the States."

"Those are elements often found in a truth serum, *cara*."

I jumped up, nearly upending my coffee mug. "A truth serum?"

Slash motioned for me to sit back down and I did, perching on the edge of the chair. "It seems as though someone might have wanted your cooperation on something, whether you were willing to give it or not."

"That's nuts."

"Not necessarily. You're an excellent hacker with enviable skills. Someone may want to use those to their advantage whether you wish to cooperate or not."

"It still doesn't make sense. Why me? You're a better hacker than me."

"That's an arguable point, but I think you already know the answer. Your skills are public, even available for hire, as part of X-Corp, whereas mine are known only to a few people most with a top-secret clearance. As you well know, to many people I don't even exist, but am a ploy by the government to dissuade potential hackers."

He had a point, especially since I had believed that before I'd met him. I exhaled a deep breath. "Okay, so what does it mean?"

"It means I'm worried. I know we can get into that

file, but I don't think we have a lot of time to play with it. We may need some help to crack open this file."

"Your contacts in the Vatican?"

"That may take too much time. I was thinking closer to home. Our home."

I looked at him in surprise. "The Zimmerman twins?"

Elvis and Xavier Zimmerman were legendary tech heads. Architects of the nation's most secretive networks, they'd recently left government employ for the more lucrative and less restrictive private sector. They were hands-down the most brilliant people I knew. Even better, they were my only friends other than Basia. More importantly, they were the only other people in the U.S., maybe even the world, capable of cracking this file and doing it quickly.

"You want me to call them?"

He nodded. "I want them to come here, if possible. I'd reimburse them for their time, of course. We could do this remotely, but we'll have a significantly better chance to crack this if all four of us are working on it together in close proximity."

"Agreed. But I don't know if they'll be able to get away on such short notice."

"We can ask."

"Okay, then. I'll call."

"Bring them up to speed. If they are able to come, tell them I'll arrange all transportation. It will be a private jet, so tell them they can bring whatever equipment they think they might need."

"Got it."

Slash handed me his phone, but I shook my head. "They won't pick up if they aren't sure who is calling. I'll use my phone."

I went back to my suitcase and dug out my phone. I had three messages from my mother. Jeez, she'd probably got my message about going to Rome and wanted to set me up with some Italian politician. I saved them for a listen-at-a-later (or never) time and pressed the button for the twins' number.

Elvis picked up on the sixth ring. "Lexi?"

"Hey, Elvis. How's it going?"

"Same old, same old. Want to come over for a game of Quake and some pizza?"

"You have no idea how much that appeals to me, but it would be kind of hard, seeing as how I'm in Rome."

There was a long silence. "You're on vacation?"

"No, I'm working. Look, that's why I'm calling. I'm kind of at an impasse on a case and wondered if you and Xavier were interested in a challenge."

"What kind of challenge?"

"Hacking."

"That's right up your alley."

"Well, it's an unusual file and I have to break it quickly. Neither Slash or I can break it."

"Slash?"

"X-Corp is on a case for his uncle."

Another long silence. "Okay, I'm interested. Use a landline and call me back at this number." He rattled off a number and I committed it to memory. "We'll be able to talk safely and securely."

He hung up and Slash raised an eyebrow. "I need a landline."

He led me down the kitchen where Nonna stood at the counter rolling out dough. I plastered a perky smile on my face and tried not to look like a guilty teenager.

Slash kissed her on the cheek and gave her a one-armed hug. See, there was that kiss-on-the-cheek thing and it apparently was no big deal for Italians to do this to everyone, all the time, regardless if they were friends or relatives. Maybe that was my problem. I should have kissed him on the cheek, not the mouth. But he had been kissing me on the mouth non-stop, so how would I know which one was right?

Despite my best efforts, my cheeks flushed hot when her gaze met mine. "Uh, good morning, Nonna."

She said something and Slash translated. "She asks whether you slept well."

My cheeks grew hotter. "I slept great. All alone. By myself."

Slash grinned and translated. His grandmother shook her finger in a scolding manner at Slash and he hugged her again.

"What did you say?"

"I said we shared a memorable night of unrequited passion under her roof."

"*What*?"

He laughed. "Don't worry, *cara*. Our secret is safe with Nonna. Here's the phone." He pointed to an old-fashioned phone sitting on a round table in the kitchen's corner and then left.

Jeez. How could he? Now I couldn't even look at Nonna. I sat down on the chair and dialed Elvis's number. He picked up on the first ring.

"Lexi?"

"Yes."

"So, fill me in."

I brought him up to speed on all the happenings, including the dead body and the poison umbrella. He listened without interruption and when I finished, he whistled.

"An umbrella dart with a sedative? That's kind of ace."

"Sure, it's ace when you're watching James Bond. It's not-so-ace when it's pointed at you."

"True. Tell me about this file."

I told him everything I could think of, including all the approaches Slash and I had already employed to crack it.

"Slash wants us there?"

"He thinks we'll get the fastest results that way. He intends to reimburse you for your time and will handle all travel via a cool private jet. You can bring whatever equipment you think you'll need. I don't know if it's a good time for you, though."

"Actually, it's a very good time. Xavier and I are due for a couple of days off anyway."

"So, you'll come?"

"Tell Slash to send a car for us. We should be ready within the hour."

"You're the best. Thanks so much."

"Save those thanks until we crack the file, okay?"

"Okay."

I hung up and started to head back up the stairs when Nonna stepped directly into my path.

"Lexi?"

Uh, oh. I didn't like the way she looked at me. My cheeks burned, but I tried to act nonchalant, like I got caught every day rolling around on the floor with guys. No big deal.

"*Si*, Nonna?"

She said something in Italian and then to my horror pointed at my privates, and said, "Lexi want bambino?"

My mouth dropped open and I pointed at myself. "Me? What? No, no. Oh. My. God. You've *so* got the wrong idea about Slash and me." I frantically made a scissor gesture in front of my stomach. "Me. Slash. No bambino. Lexi, no, no, no, with Slash."

She frowned and made a gesture to indicate a protruding stomach. I recoiled.

"Jeez. No, Nonna, no. Seriously? Oh, God, I'm really not having this conversation."

I laughed like a maniacal woman and rushed past her and up the stairs.

I bolted into the room just as Slash walked away from the printer holding up a photo of Alex Rogolli. "We've got him."

I forgot all about my encounter with Nonna. "You did? Who is he?"

"James Arthur Rutgon, age twenty-seven, unmarried and no children. U.S. citizen with a last known residence in San Diego, California."

"San Diego? Know anything else?"

"Shortly." He sat down at one of the laptops and began typing. Minutes later he sat back.

"He graduated with a BA in Chemistry at UC San Diego and then attended the Skaggs School of Pharmacy and Pharmaceutical Sciences."

"Pharmaceutical Sciences?"

"Current data says he's employed by the pharmaceutical giant, Maisto."

"Never heard of them. Who are they?"

Slash read from the screen. "A global leader in the research, development and distribution of chemically-derived pharmaceuticals." He turned and looked at me over his shoulder. "They're an Italian firm."

"Well, that adds an interesting dimension."

"They have an office in San Diego, but their headquarters are in Rome."

"Rome?" Even more interesting. "How do they play into all this if at all?"

Slash shrugged. "Too early to say. Let's keep digging. What did the twins say?"

"Send a car. They'll be ready within the hour."

"Good work." He stood and opened his cell.

I sat down in his still-warm chair. "I'm going to take a deeper look at James Rutgon."

"Knock yourself out."

He stepped out in the hall to make travel plans for the twins while I dug around in Rutgon's life.

When Slash came back into the room, I motioned for him to sit. "James Rutgon is a lot more than just a chemistry student."

Slash raised an eyebrow.

"He's a hacker. A good one. He's got a rap sheet."

Slash frowned. "He was arrested?"

"At least once. But released for lack of evidence. Guess where he was hacking?"

"A bank?"

"Bingo."

Slash picked up his coffee mug and drank what was certainly stone cold liquid by this point. To his credit, he didn't flinch. "Do you have a current location?"

"Negative. Not yet. But I'm going to check him out. I want to take a look at his past hacks. See if I can trace his signature to the one at the Vatican Bank."

"Good. I want to know how he ended up working for Maisto and what does he do."

Two hours later we had compiled probably everything there was to know about James Rutgon. Most of it wasn't good. He was a handsome and brilliant student, but with anti-social behaviors bordering on psychotic. He'd been arrested not once, but four times for hacking, twice into banks and twice into a company's account where his ex-girlfriend worked. He'd got off all four times for lack of evidence. He spoke fluent Italian and French and held a black belt in karate. He'd been recruited by Maisto about a year ago. Neither Slash nor I could account for his employment for the two years previous to that. His hacking skills were good. Really good. He had talent and flair. But he was also arrogant and careless. We were better, and with the Zimmerman twins on board, he didn't have a chance. As long as he didn't get lucky. That was statistically improbable, but unfortunately, not impossible.

Slash handed me a plate loaded with croissants, diced ham and cheese. "Courtesy of Nonna."

"Yeah, about that. I meant to tell you. I don't think she likes me."

"She adores you."

"No, I really don't think so."

Before he could say anything more, we heard a loud noise and some voices downstairs. Slash pulled his gun from his holster and headed out in the hallway. I followed. We crept into the kitchen where Nonna was talking in an animated fashion to someone. Slash holstered his gun and stepped into the kitchen with me on his heels.

"Bianca?" he said.

Chapter Nine

Bianca turned and gave Slash a melting smile with her big pouty lips. She was dressed in black ankle boots, black leather pants and a tight white sweater. If she moved funny, she might just pop out of the whole outfit.

"Angelico." She tossed her hair back, strode across the floor and practically devoured his mouth. Somehow I had a feeling the show was for me, and I was woman enough to say I didn't like it much. At least it looked like Nonna liked it even less.

Slash disengaged and began speaking to her rapidly in Italian. I don't think she liked much what he said as she argued with him, gesturing and stomping her feet.

Nonna held on to every word of the unfolding drama, whatever she'd been baking completely forgotten. After a few minutes, Bianca softened her tone with Slash, almost pleading. He leaned against the counter, listening, but barely saying anything. When it was clear Bianca wouldn't get whatever it was she wanted, she whirled on her feet and stormed out, tossing a fierce glare my way. Either Italian women had a universal lock on this drama thing or I brought out the worst in them.

After the door slammed, Nonna launched into her own tirade with Slash. He sighed, pulled her close and kissed her on the cheek. That seemed to mollify her because she clucked her tongue and went back to baking.

Slash glanced over at me. "The SIMSI sent Bianca. They got word of what's going on. They want in."

"In where?"

Slash smiled. "Exactly. At this stage there can only be a few players. Bianca is understandably upset, but she'll stay out of it for now as long as we keep her, and them, appraised."

"Will we?"

Slash shook his head. "Probably not. But if she knows we're here, so does everyone else. We're going to move to a hotel, where I can take better security precautions. Besides, with the twins and Basia coming, it's going to be too crowded for us here anyway. I'll reserve a couple of suites for us at the *Hotel Corallo.*"

I stared at him. "Basia is coming?"

"Sorry, *cara*, I forgot to tell you. I asked Finn to send her. She speaks fluent Italian and it might be beneficial to have her around in case I'm otherwise preoccupied."

I didn't know what else he'd be preoccupied with, but I was beyond thrilled Basia would be coming. She was my eyes and ears in social situations and the way things were headed with Slash, I was desperate for her guidance.

I threw my arms around his neck and gave him a hug. "That's great news, Slash. It's a really, really good idea."

He smiled. "Glad I could be accommodating. Now, let me talk to Nonna. She's not going to be happy our visit was so short."

"Okay. I'll start packing up our stuff."

I headed upstairs and re-packed the few items I'd taken out of my suitcase. I headed back into the sewing room. Slash was already there, unplugging the computers.

"That was a short talk."

"She's disappointed, but she understands it's to help Benedetto."

Truthfully, I was relieved to be leaving Nonna's house. I was sure she didn't like me and thought I was leading Slash down the road of perdition (like I even knew where it was located), the cat peed on the floor when I came around, and if I stayed, I'd weight two-hundred pounds in under a week, and *that* was a conservative estimate.

We'd become adept at setting up and packing our equipment, so it didn't take us that long to get everything ready to go. Slash went to retrieve his things and I carried my suitcase downstairs. Nonna was cooking something in the kitchen and it smelled really good.

She waved me over and held up a breaded roll with something inside. I went to take it, but realized my hands were dirty from all the packing. "Just a minute. *Momento.*"

I dashed over to the bathroom to wash my hands. I'd just turned on the water when a meow sounded from beneath the sink.

"Oh, no, you don't." I peered under the sink and saw Principessa standing next to the litter box, cleaning a paw.

"You'd better not even think about peeing on the floor again. I didn't even do anything to you and now everyone thinks I'm a cat terrorizer."

Principessa stalked out from under the sink, circled twice in front of the toilet and peed on the floor.

I stared at the cat in shock. "No way. Really?"

There was no way I was going to tell Nonna that her

perfect cat peed again on the floor, so I unrolled the toilet paper and started mopping up the pee. I dropped the soggy mess in the toilet and flushed, but it still stunk like urine in the bathroom.

"Crap." I looked around the bathroom for bleach or something equivalent to an air freshener. All I saw was what looked like a bottle of perfume. I picked it up, sniffed it, and then coughed. Jeez. It reeked like some flowers or something. But there was no question it would definitely cover up the urine smell. I sprayed it around the toilet and on the floor. In moments, the bathroom stunk so badly, I couldn't breathe. I realized all the clothes drying in the bathroom would probably stink, too. Crappola. Holding my breath, I put the perfume back, washed my hands, and went out of the bathroom leaving the door open for ventilation purposes.

I went to the kitchen, cheerfully picked up the breaded roll and popped it in my mouth. It melted on my tongue. That's when I realized Nonna was staring at me.

I stopped chewing. "What?"

She sniffed the air and I realized I probably reeked like the perfume. I waved my hand around. "Um, I thought it was air freshener."

Slash stepped into the kitchen and wrinkled his nose. "What is that smell?"

"Um, perfume. I found it in the bathroom."

Slash raised an eyebrow and I stared back with my best I'm-totally-not-guilty-of-whatever-you're-thinking look.

Nonna darted off to the bathroom and I closed my eyes. Jeez, I would never, *ever* go to the bathroom in her house again. When she came back, she held the bottle of perfume. I hoped to God it didn't have some priceless or sentimental value and I had just sprayed it on cat pee. It would *so* totally be my luck.

She held it up and asked me something in Italian.

Slash translated. "She wants to know if this is the perfume you used."

"Only if it doesn't cost a million dollars or have special sentimental value."

Slash said something to his grandmother and she pressed it into my hands.

I glanced over at Slash. "Huh?"

Slash smiled. "She wants you to have it. She's honored that you like the scent."

"Like it?" I looked down at the bottle. "Ah, jeez, that's really nice, but I couldn't possibly accept a present like this." I shoved the bottle back at her. "Thank you, but you keep it. Really."

Nonna pushed it back at me. Slash crossed his arms against his chest. He was trying not to laugh. Again.

"She insists, *cara*. Take it. You'll hurt her feelings."

I sighed, took the bottle and pretended to take a sniff. I almost gagged, but managed a smile. "Lovely. Thanks, Nonna. *Grazie*. I'll treasure it."

She beamed at me. I stuffed the bottle in the front pocket of my jeans as Nonna pressed my face between her hands and kissed both my cheeks. I turned bright red.

Jeez.

Slash walked up beside me acting all normal, but I could tell he was holding his breath. "See, I told you she likes you."

"Right."

"The cat peed on the floor again?"

I looked at him in surprise. "You knew?"

He laughed. "You have such little faith in my deductive skills. It wounds me. Come, *cara*, let's get the stuff loaded."

Sighing, I helped him load the equipment back into the car. It seemed I'd been doing a lot of this lately. Once we were packed, Slash and I said our good-byes to Nonna, who looked ready to cry.

She handed me a covered plate that was still warm. I peeked underneath the foil and saw a cake that looked like it was covered with whipped cream, black cherries and candied fruit. It smelled beyond delicious.

I forgot all about hackers, secret archives and bank thieves and just stared at the food. "Oh, my God. What is it? It looks incredible and smells even better."

Slash lifted the foil and smiled. "Sicilian cassata. One of my favorites."

I just stared at it. "It's amazing. No, it's beyond amazing. Nonna should get an honorary medal of Italy or something. How can she cook like this? It's unnatural—perhaps supernatural even."

Slash put his hand in the small of my back, pushing me toward the car. "She's Italian."

I looked at him. "Is it genetic? Can you can cook like this?"

He laughed. "Not like this. But I'm not half bad. I will show you sometime, *cara*. You'd be amazed what I can do with whipped cream."

"Excellent. I love whipped cream."

He chuckled and held the cake while I climbed into the car and buckled my seatbelt. He climbed in, opened all the windows, and off we drove.

We drove to the hotel and Slash checked us in. People were avoiding me. Slash again declined staff assistance with our equipment, for which I'm sure the bellboy was eternally grateful, and we hauled it up using a trolley.

Slash had reserved a three-bedroom suite with a large common room and a gorgeous balcony that faced the sea. I opened the balcony door and stood at the rail, smelling the ocean.

"It's beautiful. I hope we get to spend more than just a few hours here."

He came and stood beside me, putting a hand on my shoulder. "I can always bring you back sometime when we aren't working."

"I wouldn't mind seeing Tiberius's Grotto."

"It can be arranged."

"Right. But first things first."

"Absolutely. You take a shower while I set up. You stink."

"Hey, that's not what I meant."

"Trust me, it's not open for negotiation." He steered me toward the bathroom.

I sniffed my arm. I almost didn't smell it anymore. "Do I really smell that bad?"

"Worse."

"Jeez."

I took a shower, washed my hair, and changed clothes. When I came out, Slash had finished setting up the equipment and was just starting to re-initiate the protocols to crack the big file. I watched as he modified the protocol a bit and wondered whether it would help.

I sighed. "We really need to make some headway on that file."

"Agreed. Let's get something to eat and then we attack it simultaneously. I've got a few new ideas."

"Ace. Sounds like a plan."

Slash ordered *tacchino al latte*, a roasted turkey breast cooked in milk, with a side of *insalata caprese*—freshly sliced tomatoes with mozzarella cheese and basil leaves from room service. I absolutely could not stop from stuffing my face. It was delicious. However, Nonna had spoiled me to some degree. While it was delicious, it didn't taste quite as amazing as her homemade cooking. So, for dessert, we ate Nonna's cake. I had two slices and my life was complete. Seriously, I could've died a happy person with a full stomach. Go ahead. Bring on the poison darts.

Slash also ordered a bottle of wonderful Italian wine, but I held to my promise of having no more than one glass. There was *no* way I wanted a repeat of my impaired thinking from the night before. Well, truthfully, I wanted it, but I was too chicken to admit it and too scared where it might lead. Besides, Basia would be coming soon and I *really* needed her interpretation of events and advice on what to do next.

After dinner, Slash and I each sat in front of a laptop and started our concentrated attack. Now that we knew we were dealing with deniable encryption, at least we had an angle. It didn't mean it would be easy or even work.

We concentrated our efforts for several hours when we heard an unexpected knock on the door. Slash and I exchanged glances. He approached the door with his hand on his gun and looked through the peephole.

"Tito."

I rose from my chair as Slash opened the door. I waved at him. "Hey, Tito. Great to see you again."

He walked in carrying a small black duffel bag. "Glad you are still alive, my friends."

I patted my stomach. "Yeah, and at least twenty pounds heavier after all this amazing Italian food."

"I've arranged to have a few days off."

Slash nodded. "Good. We could use your help."

He sat on the couch and Slash and I quickly brought him up to speed on the latest events. He stopped us a few times and asked for clarification. Slash obliged, explaining it in German. At some point, I told him about the Zimmerman twins and Basia, who would be arriving within the next twelve hours or so to supplement the team.

Slash put Tito to work discovering whatever he could about the pharmaceutical giant Maisto while Slash and I resumed our efforts to crack the file. Hours flew past and at some point, we broke for a few hours of sleep. I don't think any of us slept well. I dreamt of numbers and code. After I awoke, I planted myself back in front of the computer to continuing my cracking. I didn't look up from the monitor until Slash's cell rang, shattering my concentration. He rose from his spot, stretching as he answered it.

He listened, said something in Italian and then tossed his phone back on the table. "They're here."

I looked up. "As in, Italy?"

"As in, downstairs."

Minutes later, Basia, Elvis, Xavier and I were hugging and high-fiving each other. We introduced them to Tito and Basia eyed him appreciatively. Jeez. I hoped Xavier didn't notice. Basia and Xavier were sort of dating, but they were not exclusive. Well, by *they* I mean Basia. She was a bit of a free spirit and in no way ready to settle down with anyone yet, even in a dating mode.

Now she stood on the balcony, listening to the sound of the ocean. "God, I love Italy." She looked pretty in black leggings, a pink sweater and dangly pink earrings. Her short dark hair was perfectly combed and her eyes were bright and sparkling. She didn't look remotely jet-lagged or tired. It didn't seem fair.

"Slash, that was the most incredible flight I've ever been on." She bounced back into the room. "The champagne was beyond exquisite."

Slash dipped his head. "I hope the trip was not too tiring. I appreciate you coming on such short notice."

"Anytime. Really."

Elvis was already examining our computer set up. "Where can we add our stuff?"

I spread my arms. "Wherever you want."

I didn't bother to ask them if they wanted to rest first. Geeks are geeks. I understood them perfectly. They were more than just a little bit excited to confront a challenge that neither Slash nor I could conquer yet.

Elvis and Xavier began unpacking their stuff and hooking it up to ours. Basia brought her stuff into my room and started unpacking. At some point we had to bring another desk out from one of the suites to add to our computer nerve center. After it was all said and done, we had enough equipment to launch a nuclear missile. Xavier had brought along a portable a/c unit and aimed it at one cluster. Elvis had set up the other cluster and Slash linked the three of them together. Whatever was in that file would be ours within a few hours.

Basia stretched out on the couch and quickly fell asleep, her face smashed into one of the cushions. I don't know how she did it, but she looked beautiful and delicate even in sleep. Xavier covered her with a blanket. He really liked her. I didn't understand their relationship or know how Xavier dealt with her free spirit or fathom how Basia juggled more than one man. I had enough social problems on my own plate to worry too much about it. I liked Xavier a lot, so I hoped it all worked out or at the very least, no one got too hurt.

I caught the twins up on all the latest developments

and after a heated hacking strategy discussion, we decided that three of us would attack the encrypted file at the same time, each of us seeking penetration at a different angle. The fourth person would monitor the clusters and rotate in when one of us got tired. Tito would continue his background search on Maisto and James Rutgon's connection to them.

Elvis, Slash and I took the first rotation. We sat in front of the computers with me in the middle. Xavier monitored the other clusters. For the most part, we worked in silence, but every now and then Slash glanced at Elvis and Elvis glanced at Slash. Not at the screen, but at each other's face. No one looked at me at all.

We worked for hours, rotating the terminals between us. Xavier sat in for Elvis, Elvis relieved me, and I gave Slash a break. Tito lasted until about one in the morning and then he crashed in Slash's suite. I managed to stay awake on sheer adrenaline. The twins and Slash were operating on the same biophysical high. There was nothing more thrilling in the world for a geek than a seemingly insurmountable hack because we all knew that nothing was insurmountable. It was a game of matching wits, skill and sheer persistence.

When she awoke, Basia provided us with coffee and breakfast. None of us wanted to take a break yet. We still hadn't cracked the file, but we were making progress. Really good progress. I'd just sat down in the chair Xavier had vacated when Elvis sat up straight.

"Hello. I've got entry, people."

Slash stopped typing and leaned over, almost on top of me. His five o'clock shadow had moved into beard territory, but his dark eyes gleamed excitedly. Xavier, Basia and Tito crowded behind Elvis's chair.

"How?" Slash asked.

"Buffer overflow."

"Optimum," breathed Xavier.

"What's a buffer overflow?" Basia asked.

I peered at Elvis's screen. "He tricked the memory into dumping so he could inject a code that would permit him to perform a task at a higher level than he's authorized. He just authorized himself in and apparently it worked."

"I'm in, but we don't have the file yet," Elvis warned.

I shrugged. "It's just a matter of time now."

Elvis's hands flew across the screen, a lock of his dark hair falling across his forehead. Slash and I had abandoned our efforts and simply watched Elvis at work. I understood only about half of what he was doing. Slash understood a lot more because he offered advice a few times when Elvis paused. Eventually Basia and Tito got bored and sat on the balcony sipping coffee and chatting.

Two and half hours later Elvis finally said, "Bingo."

Xavier, Slash and I had stayed with Elvis, keeping him awake, helping him when he stalled. Still, when Elvis said it, I started in my chair and wondered if I'd been dozing with my eyes open.

Elvis rose, glancing at Slash. "You have the honors, dude." He switched chairs with Slash. "I don't know what's in there, but that was one heck of a hack and you and Lexi had already taken care of most of the legwork."

I gave Elvis a tired smile and he patted my shoulder. Tito and Basia joined us as we all leaned over to see what had been so expertly encrypted.

Slash clicked and the screen filled with a large image.

"A photo?" I said in surprise.

Slash adjusted the image, scaling it down so we could better see it. "A photo of a painting."

"*Quadro*. The name of the file."

I squinted at it. A full-figured naked woman had her hands raised to the heavens while a white-bearded man frowned down at her from the sky. The sky looked as if it were on fire with angry slashes of red and purple. The woman sat on a rock in a forest, a blanket of colorful flowers spread artfully across her lap.

Slash glanced over his shoulder. "Anyone recognize this?"

Elvis shook his head. "No, but the style looks familiar. Renaissance period for sure."

"Agreed." Slash kept refining the picture, making it smaller, easier to view.

Xavier peered closer. "Is the artist's name on the painting?"

Slash did a cursory glance and then magnified the image to search all the corners. "I don't see anything."

Apparently my education was lacking in the fine arts department. "What does it mean?"

Slash shook his head. "I'm not sure yet. We need to go hunting in some art databases and see if we can locate this painting."

"If it's from the secret Vatican archives, will it be in a database?"

"Probably not. But we have to eliminate the possibility."

Crankiness reared its ugly head. This is what we hacked for numerous days and hours? A freaking painting?

I let out a big huff. "So, why would a painting be in a secret archive in the first place? Art is art. Shouldn't it be on display somewhere?"

"Obviously we can't know the answer to that at this point."

Elvis rolled his neck. "Well, at the least we might be able to determine the painter if we can pinpoint similar paintings or specific techniques."

I should have thought of that and I wanted to mull more on it, but my brain was on complete shutdown. The exhilaration of the hack had passed. I looked around and saw bleary eyes, mussed hair and gray pallor. We all needed to sleep and refresh our minds.

I decided to be the bigger man and fold first. "We need to sleep. Now. Everyone."

Elvis rubbed his eyes. "Agreed."

Slash ran his fingers through his hair. I couldn't remember seeing him so tired. "*Si.* I'm just going to start an automatic search in some databases and I'm finished."

We left Tito and Basia in charge of monitoring the database search. I dragged myself to the bathroom where I washed my face, brushed my teeth and put on my pajamas. I crawled in bed and pulled the sheet to my chin. I usually like to reflect on my day right before I go to sleep, but I closed my eyes and that's the last thing I remembered.

Chapter Ten

Coffee. I smelled coffee. I rolled over, opened my eyes and took a moment to get oriented. Where the heck was I?

Oh, yes. Italy. In a hotel in Sperlonga. We were working on an encrypted file...correction, we'd *cracked* an encrypted file only to find a photo of an old painting. Jeez. I almost got shot by a poison umbrella gun for *that*?

I sat up and saw the bed was empty. I had no idea where Basia was and how long I'd slept. I jumped out of bed and threw on a pair of jeans and a T-shirt. I ran my fingers through my hair. Barefoot, I wandered out to into the common room. Basia and Slash sat in front of the computers. Well, Basia sat sideways in the chair watching Slash, sipping coffee and looking as gorgeous and rested as if she'd just been to a spa. It wasn't fair. She was supposed to be jet-lagged or at least have some circles under her eyes.

Xavier, Elvis and Tito were nowhere to be found, presumably still asleep. Slash smiled at me when I came in and patted the chair next to him.

"Good morning, *cara*."

"Is it morning?"

Basia laughed. "Actually it's about five in the afternoon. You guys went to bed at eight in the morning."

I smiled. "Hacker hours."

Slash smiled back as Basia handed me a cup of coffee. "Are you hungry, Lexi?"

"I'm perpetually hungry in Italy."

"I'm not surprised. The food is terrific. I'm getting ready to go out and get something for us to munch on until dinner."

"Sure, whatever."

She grabbed her coat and headed out. I dared a sip of coffee and realized Basia had watered it down for me. Thank God for best friends.

I studied Slash's face. He'd showered, shaved and smelled really good. Again. "So, did you get any sleep?"

"Some. I've been up for a bit studying the painting."

"Any stunning revelations?"

"No hits in any of the main art databases. I think we can safely assume this is not a well-known painting. However, I may have narrowed the list of potential artists. It's likely a protégé of Leonardo da Vinci."

"But not Leonardo himself?"

"I don't think so. Da Vinci's paintings are all very distinct because he used a technique called velature. He didn't mix colors on the palette like most artists of his time. Instead he painted by applying layers of paint on top of each other to create a special kind of texture and depth of color."

I learned something new every day when I hung around geek guys. "Cool. His protégés didn't do this?"

"Apparently it was a difficult technique to do well. All his protégés used it to one extent or another…but very sparingly."

"I take that to mean this painting shows evidence of velature, just not an expertise using the technique."

"*Si.*"

I sipped my coffee and thought it over. "Okay. I'm still not sure how that ties into anything."

"We'll figure it out." He tapped on the screen. "Whatever we need to know is right here somewhere. This is a pure digital copy of the real painting, taken with a special camera. Presumably this is to protect the painting from forgers or thieves and also to assure it could be repaired to its exact genuine state if damaged in any way."

"And that's important because...?"

"With a special photograph like this, someone could study the painting down to the tiniest of pixels."

I ventured a guess. "And make a really good hi-tech forgery."

"*Si*. But ultimately it would not fool the experts. Not with the technology these days. So, I don't think we should head down that path."

I sighed, frustrated. Frankly, it had been a real letdown to see what was in the file. Plus my knowledge of art was less than stellar and I felt adrift without something to hack or calculate.

Perhaps sensing my disappointment, Slash put his hand over mine and gave it a squeeze. "There's got to be something else here, *cara*. I just feel it. It's in the secret archives for a reason. I'm just not getting the forgery vibe."

There was a noise behind us. "Just what vibe *are* you getting?"

Elvis stood there in a white undershirt and a pair of jeans. He was barefoot like me and his dark hair stood straight up as if he'd stuck his finger in an electrical socket. He had dark rings under his eyes and I realized how tired he must be after flying all day and then working all night.

Slash released my hand and stood. "Good morning, my friend."

Elvis didn't look happy. I guess jet lag wasn't agreeing with him.

I picked up my coffee cup. "We've got some news. Slash narrowed down the list of potential artists. They are da Vinci's protégés. Apparently this is a special photograph taken with a special camera that permits us to see every little pixel of the painting if we want."

"Why would we want to?"

"Maybe there is something useful there for us to see."

Slash nodded. "I've already taken a cursory look, but saw nothing out of the ordinary."

Elvis sat in the chair next to me. "Let me take a look."

"Want some coffee?"

"Sure. Milk and sugar. Lots of it."

We were two peas in a pod. I poured coffee in a mug, adding a generous amount of milk and sugar. Elvis took a sip and winced. There you have it. Americans and Italian coffee just don't go together. No further experimentation necessary.

I scooted my chair closer to his. "I'll take a look with you. The more eyes the better."

"Actually, I've got a better idea." Slash reached over Elvis and typed some commands. "There. I've made copies of the file. I'll send them out to the other laptops and we can all take a look at it from our own terminals and from different angles. Maybe we'll get lucky."

For a moment, Elvis met Slash's eyes, but no one said

anything as I moved my chair back to my terminal and started to study my copy of the photograph.

By the time Basia arrived with food and fresh coffee, Tito and Xavier were both up and sitting in front of laptops, examining the painting. I made a station for Basia, too. She complained she didn't know what she was looking for, but I told her to examine the picture as a whole. Maybe the way the woman sat or the way the guy from the sky looked at her was some kind of secret message. The alignment of the trees or the scratches on the rock could be significant. She rolled her eyes, but really did put in a lot of effort despite playing footsies with Xavier.

Three hours later my eyesight had started to swim from looking at all the pixels. I leaned back in my chair, rubbing my eyes. "It's like looking for a needle in a haystack. I've eliminated the dark pixels, the light pixels, the blue, green and red pixels, separately and in succession, blacked out the background, overexposed the background, and gone over every freaking inch of this painting. *Nada.*"

Basia stood and stretched her hands over her head. "I've got nothing, too. Nothing seems suspect or as if it's conveying a message. Truthfully, I don't even know what I'm looking for. It's worse than looking for a needle in a haystack because, at least in that case, I know I'm looking for a needle."

Tito sighed. "I'm with both of them. *Nichts.*"

Elvis rolled his neck. "I played with differing degrees of focus but didn't see anything interesting. I reduced and then enlarged the face, the body, the sky, the flowers, the trees, the rock and her breasts. There's nothing there I can see."

Xavier snickered when Elvis said breasts.

Elvis shot him a dirty look. "Dork."

Xavier shrugged, too busy admiring Basia as she did a couple of yoga moves to stretch out. After a moment he sighed and leaned back in his chair, linking his fingers behind his neck. "Well, I worked the rotation angle. I rotated everything six ways to Sunday and found zip."

We all looked hopefully to Slash who shook his head.

"I looked for significant clues or meanings to the items in the painting. I didn't find anything that made sense. I did track down the type of camera used to photograph the painting. It's a high-end digital SLR camera with interchangeable lenses, mostly likely a Hasselblad H4D-60, one of the most expensive digital cameras in the world. Costly, but the purpose is photographing priceless works of art after all. It's no coincidence they are using this same camera for cataloguing the digital inventory in the Vatican archives. Therefore, it's a logical extrapolation that they'd use this for the secret archives, too."

I blew out a frustrated breath. "So, why the heck is a painting hidden in the depths of the Vatican secret archives? How secret should a painting be? Maybe I've been wrong all along and I overlooked something else on Serafina's hard drive."

Slash pushed away from the terminal and went to the French doors that led out to the balcony. He pulled open the doors and stood looking out at the ocean. After a minute, he turned around. "No. You took the right files, *cara*. Whatever we need, it's either in this painting or it's connected with it."

Elvis nodded. "I'm with Slash. There has to be some major significance to this file. That was no ordinary encryption. It's one of the heaviest I've ever encountered and I've encountered plenty. There's definitely something up with this painting. We just can't see it yet."

I liked how he added *yet* to the end of his sentence. If it were here, whatever *it* was, I knew Elvis would find it.

"Okay. Then what's next?" I stood and touched my toes, stretching out the muscles in my back and legs.

Slash sat back down at the terminal and flexed his fingers. "We keep looking. All of us."

Exhaustion set in a few hours later and Basia insisted we take a break for dinner. Technically we were no closer to discovering the mystery of the photograph than when we started. Xavier had designed a program on one of the smaller clusters to run some algorithms to determine if there were any unusual patterns in the pixel placement and to analyze the lighting. He checked on it occasionally while we all sat on the floor of the suite, around a large glass coffee table. We dined on excellent Italian food ordered from room service. There was *zuppa di cozze*, a fish soup, and *scaloppini di Vitello*, delicious breaded scallops. Several bottles of superb Italian wine accompanied the dinner and I drank more than one glass, seeing as how my best friend and social director sat next to me. I felt a lot more relaxed knowing that I could count on her for proper guidance, plus it was beyond unlikely I'd be left alone with anyone to make a fool of myself. Besides, the wine loosened me up a bit, made me a little less mentally rigid. Sometimes that worked for me in terms of ideas. Bank fraud, dead bodies, and a painting with a naked lady could take a hike, at least for a while.

Xavier asked Basia her favorite line from a movie. She scrunched up her forehead, thinking. "That's a hard question."

"I know mine," Elvis said, lifting his wineglass. "It's from the Matrix when Morpheus is talking to Neo, trying to convince him to leave the artificial world and enter reality. He says, 'You've felt it your entire life, that there's something wrong with the world. You don't know what it is, but it's there, like a splinter in your mind, driving you mad.'"

I nodded with approval. "Excellent."

"Here's mine." Xavier put a hand on his chest. "I'm putting myself to the fullest possible use, which is all I think that any conscious entity can ever hope to do."

"Hal, the computer," I said, smiling. "2001 A Space Odyssey."

Tito lifted his wine glass. "Can anyone guess this?" He deepened his voice and added an Italian accent. "I'm going to make him an offer he can't refuse."

"Sweet." Elvis clinked his wine glass with Tito. "Don Corleone in *The Godfather.*"

"Okay, okay, I've got mine." Basia stood up, swaying a bit and then taking a dramatic stance. "The world… is my oyster." She collapsed, giggling. I started laughing as well.

"That's not from a movie." Xavier frowned.

"No, it's not." Slash set aside his wineglass and stood. "Shakespeare. *The Merry Wives of Windsor.*"

I looked at him in surprise. Slash knew Shakespeare? I guess I shouldn't be surprised, he apparently knew everything about anything, regardless of language, country or culture.

Basia fluttered her eyelashes at him. "Come on now, Mr. Dark and Mysterious. It's your turn."

"I don't have time to watch movies."

"Don't be a party pooper," she insisted, tipping her

wineglass toward him, the wine sloshing. "You've got to have at least one."

I thought he'd ignore her, but instead he looked over at me, his expression darkening. In a spot-on imitation of Humphrey Bogart, he said, "Of all the gin joints, in all the towns, in all the world, she walks into mine."

He said it with such perfect emphasis and emotion that everyone was struck silent.

I spoke first. "Wow, Slash. That was un-freaking-believable. An amazing impersonation of the late, great Bogart. If the national security thing doesn't work out, you would be a great voice talent. Right, guys?" I looked around the room.

Basia cleared her throat, looking decidedly uncomfortable. "Ah, sure. Great movie, that *Casablanca*."

Slash gave a slight bow, walked over to the balcony and stared out into the darkness. Basia looked at me and raised an accusing eyebrow, as if I could magically interpret the meaning of that. When I gave her a puzzled look, she frowned, which left me wondering what had just happened.

Elvis abruptly stood and disappeared into his room. Tito started chuckling as Xavier grabbed the bottle of wine, filling up his glass. Sighing, I picked up my wine and took a large gulp. Why was I always the clueless one during social conversations? Even the twins seemed to have sensed something. I'd have to ask her later for a translation, if we had five minutes alone to talk. Something had just killed the mood and apparently I was the culprit.

Xavier topped off Basia's wineglass and asked me if I wanted more. I shook my head. My buzz was fading. Slash stared moodily out the window, Elvis had gone, and I didn't feel like playing any more. I was tired and discouraged that we were making so little progress on the painting. It had been so freaking hard to crack open and the payoff had been…nothing.

Basia took another sip of her wine and sighed. "Okay. I admit it. I cheated. My favorite movie line is really from Moonstruck when Nicholas Cage tells Cher that he—"

I sat straight up. "Wait, wait. Did you say Nicholas Cage?"

Basia looked at me. "Yes. As in the actor."

I smacked my forehead. "Nicholas Cage. That's it."

"What's it? Lexi, are you drunk?"

"National Treasure."

"Sure, it was an okay movie for an action/adventure, but it's important because…?"

I bolted to my feet and raced over to the computer. Slash looked away from the window, watching me. I sat down, my hands flying over the keyboard. Slash came to stand behind me and Xavier and Basia crowded around, as well.

"Lexi, what on earth are you doing?" Basia asked.

"Give me a few minutes." I created a copy of the photo and flipped it.

Slash's fingers curled over the back of the chair, pressing into my back. His warmth steadied me as I slowly began to transpose one photo on top of the other.

Xavier leaned closer. "What are you doing, geek queen?"

"She's superimposing." Elvis spoke. He'd apparently returned to the room and came to stand by my right side. "Ingenious."

I shrugged. "Only if it works."

Basia frowned. "Superimposing? I'm a translator and

I still don't know what you guys are talking about. Can someone please speak freaking English?"

Xavier patted her arm. "She made a copy of the photo and is putting it on top of itself."

"If she puts the same picture on top of itself, how will that help? Won't it blend into itself?"

I opened the original photo file. "It won't blend if I flip the copy first."

"Flip?"

"Turn it backwards. Then superimpose it."

"Optimum." Elvis leaned closer to the monitor, studying the photo as well.

"Okay, so do I have to be the one to ask the obvious question first?" Basia lifted her hands in the air. "What on God's green earth does any of this have to do with Nicholas Cage?"

I grinned in spite of myself. "*National Treasure*, the movie. Cage starred in it. Don't you remember when he was searching for the mythical treasure, he found clues in historical artifacts like the dollar bill and the Declaration of Independence?"

"I'm still not following."

"He transposed, superimposed and manipulated images to reveal clues hidden in historical artifacts by the very people who created them. When you said 'Cage' it reminded me of the movie, and then it reminded me of the strategies he took to uncover the clues hidden in historically important items. Superimposing, for example. It's a simple but an effective way to hide an important clue in a photo or an image. More importantly, it wasn't that hard to do even back in older times. All you had to do was use a mirror."

Xavier whistled. "You really think this might work?"

"You got a better idea?"

"Not at all."

"So, let's give it a shot."

I slid on my glasses and kept my hand steady on the mouse as I slowly pulled the other photo across.

"It needs to go a little to the left." Elvis pointed to a red, red, green pixel set.

I followed his instructions and dragged it left. After another minute, the photo was flipped and fully superimposed over the original. "Alright." I exhaled a breath I hadn't know I was holding. "Let's take a look now."

I magnified the photo to about 500 percent and everyone leaned over to peer at the screen. Slash murmured to himself in Italian while we went micro inch by micro inch across the screen. I stared so hard, the colors started to bleed together. Twice I had to close my eyes to clear them.

After a few minutes, Xavier cried out.

"Upper left corner."

I immediately zoomed in and saw what he was talking about. My heart leapt as I clarified the picture. Numbers. It was series of freaking numbers.

Xavier whooped and Elvis gave me a high five.

I swallowed hard. "Holy Batman. We've found the Grail."

Xavier slapped me on the back. "We've got more than the Grail, Lexi. We've got numbers."

My heart soared. This hotel suite, at this very moment in time, most likely contained the world's best brains in terms of cracking numbers and code. To say that numbers were our forte would be a severe understatement.

Slash leaned down and gave me a kiss on cheek. "Good work, *cara*."

"We all did it." I stood up from my chair, smiling like a freaking idiot.

"No, *you* did it," Elvis corrected. "Good thinking."

Xavier jotted down the numbers and held them up for our scrutiny.

Tito held up his hands. "Okay, now you are all way past me. I'm not sure what just happened."

"Me, neither," said Basia.

I barely heard them. My focus was hot on those numbers. My brain searched, discarded and manipulated those numbers, looking for a pattern that made sense. Then just like that, I had it. Still, I had to be sure.

After a minute, Xavier shook his head. "Nothing is jumping out at me." He set the paper with the numbers down next to one of the laptops. None of us needed the visual anymore. We all had them memorized in a variety of different configurations. "Shall I run them through a program?"

Elvis picked up a pencil and began to jot down something. "Not necessary. Not yet anyway."

Slash also studied the numbers intently. Nobody looked at me. I glanced between the guys, wondering if I should say what I thought the numbers meant. I didn't want to appear immodest, especially in the presence of some of the most brilliant minds in the world, but I'm sure I already knew what they stood for.

Slash glanced up at me and lifted a dark eyebrow. "Okay. So, what's the translation?"

"Translation?"

"The code. The one you've already calculated in your head. The one you are trying to decide whether to tell us about or not."

Jeez. The dude was good. Either that or I had the worst poker face in the history of the universe.

Elvis looked up from whatever he was writing. "You got something, Lexi?"

I rubbed the back of my neck, suddenly nervous. What if I were epically wrong? I didn't handle embarrassment well, especially in front of my peers.

"I don't know. It's just a guess."

"Everything is a guess." Xavier pointed at me. "Give."

My gaze went back to Slash's. "Well, I'm not sure. It seems too simple. But it might be worth examining."

"The code, *cara*."

"Well, that's just it. I don't think it is code at all. I think it may be directions."

Elvis glanced down at the numbers. "Directions?"

"Longitude and latitude."

Elvis tapped his pencil on the numbers, considering. "Conceivable. Let's check it out on Google Earth."

He typed in the numbers and we all leaned over to see what popped up on the monitor.

Xavier whistled when it narrowed in. "Your brain is on fire, geek queen. It's Italy."

"Where in Italy?" I asked.

Slash asked Elvis to magnify the location. "Vaprio d'Adda."

I frowned. "Where's that?"

"It's a municipality located about thirty kilometers northeast of Milan."

"Okay, what's the significance, if any?"

Slash rubbed his chin. "Not sure. Give me a minute to think." He sat at a different terminal, typed in some commands. After a minute, he spoke. "Interesting."

"What's interesting?"

"Francesco Melzi's estate is located in Vaprio d'Adda."

"Who's Francesco Melzi?"

"A Renaissance painter."

I raised an eyebrow. "Did he happen to know da Vinci?"

"Quite well actually. Not only was he one of da Vinci's protégés, he was also the executor of his estate."

I nodded. "Interesting, indeed."

Slash flipped through a few more screens and stopped on one with a picture of a large mansion. "*Villa Melzi* is here. However, this exact latitude and longitude puts us a few kilometers away…at a cemetery to be exact."

"A cemetery?" A chill ran down my spine.

Slash frowned. "Let me check the numbers again." He leaned over the screen and re-entered the numbers. He added a few more commands and then checked on something. After a moment, he sighed and sat back in his chair, linking his fingers behind his head. "*Si*, these coordinates definitely put us at the cemetery. But it's not where Melzi is buried."

Basia leaned over Slash's shoulder. "Where's Melzi buried?"

"On his estate."

Basia shivered. "This is way too creepy. A cemetery? That can't be right."

I sat in an empty chair. "Basia's right. Maybe it's not latitude or longitude."

Slash shook his head. "No, it's right, *cara.* I feel it."

I rubbed my eyes. My eyelids felt heavy and the wine had made me sleepy again. Jetlag had finally caught up with me. My body didn't know when to sleep and when to stay up.

Xavier sat down in the chair. "We need to finish

looking at the painting. There might be something else we missed."

Elvis nodded. "Just in case."

We all sat down again and examined the painting micro inch by micro inch. None of us found anything other than those numbers, despite trying a number of other techniques similar to superimposing. Somewhere in the middle of our search, Slash got a phone call and stepped into his room to take it. Now he returned.

He slid the phone into his pocket. "Uncle Benedetto called. He's gone through the file I sent containing the financial records. They were receipts of payments from Maisto Inc. of Italy to one James Rutgon, American. These are not official payments or paychecks and the spreadsheet looks like it was created and maintained by Rutgon himself. The payments were made to offshore accounts and I'd bet he's not paying taxes on any of them. I'm going to hack in and see if any of those accounts just received a large payment of, say, nine million euros."

"Isn't financial information, like, personal?" Basia asked.

We all turned and stared at her. She lifted her hands. "Okay. Dead girl. Stolen religious money. I get it. Just saying."

I stood, snatched a croissant off a tray and took a bite. "Now the real mystery is how did it get on Serafina's hard drive?"

Elvis leaned back in his chair. "Easy. She stole it."

"Huh?" I frowned. "Dude, James Rutgon is an accomplished hacker. No way he left something this sensitive unprotected on his hard drive."

"Exactly. I'd never *leave* anything incriminating on

my hard drive because I wouldn't have *had* it there in the first place."

"Not following you." I stuffed the rest of the croissant in my mouth.

Elvis held out a hand. "Give me one of those croissants." I tossed him one and he caught it. He took a bite.

"Okay, let me put it this way, Lexi. If you were involved in an illegal activity, say hacking into a bank, and you were caught, what's the first thing the police would confiscate?"

"First of all, I wouldn't hack into a bank. Well, not to steal money anyway. And I definitely wouldn't get caught."

"We're being theoretical here."

"Fine. Of course, the police would take my computer."

"Exactly. Which means if Rutgon is good at hiding his trail, which given his hacking skills we have to presume he is, he'll have nothing incriminating on his hard drive."

"Good point." I mulled it over for a moment. Where would I keep files I didn't want anyone to see? I thought about my keychain—the one with the flash drive. Jeez, I'd put it on a separate drive, of course.

"Okay, so Rutgon hides the file on a flash drive or a soft server somewhere. He'd sure as heck encrypt it, though."

Slash perched on the corner of one of the desks. "Which is exactly what he did, *cara*."

"But how did Serafina get it? Why was it on her hard drive?

Slash shrugged. "It's hard to say. My guess is that it was on a flash drive or a portable server of some kind.

Serafina stole or borrowed it and copied the file to her hard drive."

"But she didn't know what was in it."

"Most likely not. But it is not too far-fetched to assume that she figured something important was on it."

I imagined the situation in my head. "Okay, so let's say Serafina saw a flash drive hanging on his keychain, backpack, or wherever, and wondered why he always carried it on him. When she started getting suspicious he was up to something or had used her, she stole it from him, maybe just to take a look. She couldn't open the file because of the encryption, but it was potential leverage. She dragged the file onto her hard drive at work, hoping to get someone to help her open it at a later date. Maybe she didn't realize Rutgon could access her computer at work at that point. Who knows? But eventually she must have realized it and was able to shut him out before he could retrieve or delete it from her hard drive."

Elvis popped the rest of the croissant in his mouth. "I think that's a reasonable assumption. He underestimated her."

I sighed. "This beyond sucks. Someone has to let her parents know all this someday. She was a smart, smart girl."

Tito snorted. "Not smart enough. She's dead. Just saying, yah?"

He had a point, I guess, but it still didn't seem fair she paid with her life because of lousy taste in men. It only confirmed my suspicion that relationships sucked. Not that I had any to base that theory on.

Slash ran his fingers through his hair. "Well, at this point it's clear what needs to be done next."

Tito crossed his legs. "I sure hope it's something besides staring at a computer."

Slash nodded. "We need to make a trip to Vaprio d'Adda and see what we can find at those coordinates. But tomorrow. Tonight we need to sleep."

I held up a hand. "You do realize we just got up about six hours ago."

Xavier rubbed his temples. "Personally, I'm with Slash. We need to get our bodies adjusted to this time period. I wouldn't mind a few more hours of shut eye."

Slash picked up his glass of water. "We all need to be at our best. We aren't sure what we're looking for and what we may find in that cemetery. I need time in the morning to go looking around Rutgon's accounts. I'd like to find that money. He has to have it somewhere." He took a sip. "It would also help to have a little more knowledge under our belts on Vaprio d'Adda, Francesco Melzi, and other artists of the time. Tito and Basia can gather potential supplies for the trip—shovels, ropes, flashlights and food. It takes nearly six hours to get to Vaprio d'Adda from Sperlonga. I'd like us to arrive by sunset. We'll explore the cemetery at dusk when the possibility for visitors is low. Especially since we aren't sure what we're doing or may have to do."

Basia narrowed her eyes. "I sincerely hope we aren't bringing shovels on this excursion because we're planning to dig up dead people. That's way beyond my job description."

Slash spread out his hands. "I make no promises. I don't know what we'll find at those exact coordinates. We need to be prepared for anything, including digging. X may mark the spot."

"Ugh." Basia frowned. "I was afraid you'd say that."

No one could think of any argument, including me,

so we headed off to bed. I let Basia take her shower first. After I finished, I kind of hoped we could have some girl time. I needed to bring her up to speed with what had happened with Slash and see what she thought of the situation. I put on my pjs, dried my hair and went into the bedroom. Basia was already sound asleep under the covers.

"Crappola."

Dejected, I crawled into bed, careful not to disturb her, but I had a hard time falling asleep. So many things were running through my head and it was clear my brain wasn't ready to shut down yet. Or maybe I just drank too much of the strong Italian coffee. It was hard to say. I tried various relaxing meditative techniques, reciting the chemical elements table, and calculating pi, but it was no good. Sleep was not in my immediate future.

Sighing, I stopped tossing and went into the sitting room. The balcony door was wide open, letting in a rush of cool air. There was a full moon and the light spilled over the balcony and into the living room. The sound of the ocean was calming and predictable, which is probably why I liked it, except for the sand, sun and bathing suits part. I inched closer and saw Slash sitting alone at the balcony table sipping something from a glass.

I thought I'd moved stealthily, but he said, "Care to join me, *cara?*"

Chapter Eleven

I padded out onto the balcony and shivered in the cool air. He stood, took off his jacket and draped it around my shoulders. I'd worn his jacket before and it was warm, soft and smelled good like Slash.

"Won't you be cold?"

"I'm fine."

I couldn't argue with that, as he always seemed to be radiating heat. I sat in a chair across from him and tucked my bare feet beneath me. "What are you drinking?"

"Whiskey."

"Why? I thought you were the one insisting we all go to bed."

"People need a decent amount of sleep to perform adequately and adjust their bodies to this time zone."

"Except for you."

"I need sleep, too, *cara.* Tonight I'm having trouble unwinding."

"Me, too. Which is why I'm here, I guess."

A smile touched his lips. "Would you like a drink?"

"No." I said that way too fast, so I took a breath and slowed down. "I mean, no, thanks. I'm good. Really."

For a moment, neither of us said anything and then

I sighed. "Are you worried about what we'll find at the cemetery tomorrow?"

Slash shrugged. "What will be will be."

"Then something else worries you?"

"*Si.*"

He didn't offer any more information and he didn't seem like he was in the chatty mood. I fiddled with the zipper on his jacket and tried to think of a way to distract him from worrying about whatever it was he was worried about.

"I can help you with the search on Rutgon's account tomorrow, if you want. I know you don't need the help, but if you'd like it—"

He waved a hand. "Of course I'd like it. We both know Rutgon is ours now. He won't be able to hide the information from us."

"No, he won't. It's also unlikely he'll have spent it by now."

"He might have transferred it elsewhere."

I shrugged. "Big deal. Transfers require a trail. Following a trail is no problem for us."

His smile widened. "*Si.* You are right, *cara.*" He sipped his whiskey, regarded me in the moonlight. "Let me ask you something. Why do you think Maisto paid Rutgon to complete a very difficult hack into the Vatican secret archives to obtain a photo of a painting that contained a hidden numerical code? Who knew that the code would be there and how does Maisto play into all of this?"

I lifted my hands. "Good questions, both of them. Unfortunately I don't have any answers, just a question of my own. Why the heck is this painting in the secret archives in the first place and not on display in some museum? The most logical answer would be that someone in the Vatican knew or knows about the code in the painting and possibly what it means. For some reason, the Vatican thought it worth hiding. Why?"

Slash lifted his glass, took a sip. "I don't know. It could also be that they aren't hiding it, but protecting it…whatever *it* may be."

"Good point. Well, I'm going to think positively and say we're about to find out what *it* is. We got lucky, Slash. We broke the encryption and found the code, hopefully before anyone else. At this point, we've got no other logical course of action than to follow the trail—see where it leads. Tomorrow we'll discover if I've led everyone down the wrong path. Forty lashes can commence at that time, if necessary."

For a moment he just looked at me and then he laughed softly.

I pursed my mouth. "Okay, I'm *really* starting to get a complex because you laugh at me so much."

He shook his head. "No, *cara*, I'm not laughing *at* you. I'm laughing because you relax me. Soothe me. You make me…happy."

A warm glow spread inside me. Slash and happy didn't seem like natural synonyms. To think I could contribute to a small moment of his happiness, even if it was at my expense, made me feel good.

He tossed back the rest of his whiskey and stood. "Come, *cara*, before I make a further fool of myself. We need to try to sleep at least a little."

I stood and started to wiggle out of his jacket when I felt him behind me, his hands on my shoulders, helping me take it off. The jacket zipper caught on the left sleeve of my pajama top, tugging it down and leaving my shoulder bare. I reached over to pull it up when Slash suddenly caught my wrist and held it. I started to ask him what he was doing, when he bent down and pressed his mouth against the cool skin on my shoulder. He kissed, nibbled and…oh, God, was he tasting it?

His tongue caressed, his teeth grazed my skin. I froze, every nerve ending in my body rushing to the spot where his mouth touched me. Moonlight spilled over us as he nestled me into him, pulling me back into his chest, his arm tightening around me.

He murmured against my skin. "*Mio dio*, I can't help it. I'm not a saint. I want you, *cara*."

I couldn't see his face, but somehow, not being able to see it and having him holding me from behind me was surprisingly erotic. It left me no option other than to feel. The way he kissed me, revered me, held me…

It was as if all intellectual avenues in my brain had shut down, replaced by a single-minded journey down a mysteriously sensual road. I shivered with a mixture of heat and cold as he made his way with languid expertise across my shoulder blade inch by inch. Oh, God. I *wanted* him to do more. I never *ever* wanted him to stop.

When he moved his lips into the hollow of my neck, I closed my eyes, letting my body melt back against him, even turning my neck to the side to permit him better access, like a victim to a vampire. For the first time in my life I finally got why those girls in the old-time horror movies let Dracula go at their necks with no resistance. I always thought if I were in their place, I'd turn and punch him in the nose. But now I understood. It was physiologically possible to be paralyzed by sexual magnetism. And Slash had sexual magnetism in spades. I wondered if that meant I was being ravished and decided that if it felt like this, I'd be first in line to sign up, woman's liberation or punctured necks notwithstanding.

"Lexi?"

I didn't open my eyes because I assumed it was Slash saying something and I wasn't ready to surrender the sensations. I had absolutely no shred of desire to try and bring my brain back to conversational mode, which I sucked at anyway. When I heard my name a second time, a bit louder, I opened my eyes, then jumped as Basia stepped into the balcony doorway.

"What are you doing?"

Slash turned around, bringing the leather jacket with him. Her eyes widened as she looked back and forth between us. "Oh." She cleared her throat. "Well, oh. I woke up and saw you weren't there so I…"

Her mouth dropped open and I realized my top still hung off the one shoulder where Slash had been nibbling his way to…somewhere. Jeez where had he been heading? Even more importantly, had I really cared as long as he didn't stop?

Guiltily, I jerked my sleeve over my shoulder, nearly ripping it in the process. "Um, about that. Right. See, I couldn't sleep and Slash couldn't either. Then we were… talking, yes, talking about…stuff. After a bit we decided to go to bed. But not together in the same bed. No, jeez, no. That's not what I meant. He gave me his jacket and I was giving it back when—"

Before I could continue, Slash gave me a kiss on the cheek. "Good night, *cara*." He walked past Basia and patted her once on the shoulder before disappearing into his suite.

Basia pointed at me. "Bad."

I looked over my shoulder and then back at Basia. "Bad, what?"

"Bad, he almost ate you alive."

I remembered the way I'd offered him my neck. "I know. It was…."

My eyes must have started to glaze over, because she snapped at me. "Do *not* fantasize. This is not good."

"It's not?"

"Of course it's not. This is Slash we are talking about. You haven't been *talking* with him like this the whole time you've been in Rome have you?"

"No." I paused, thinking about that moment at Nonna's house. "Well, not exactly. I've been meaning to talk to you about that. We're having this issue about doors."

Basia grabbed my arm, pulling me back out onto the balcony and lowering her voice to a hiss. "Haven't we already had this talk about the rabbit in the thrall of the wolf? He was seducing you."

For some reason, the thought of it made me happy. Slash wanted to seduce me? That meant I was seduce-worthy. Optimum.

"Focus, Lexi. Listen to me. I'll be the first to admit that Slash is gorgeous, sexy, smart and, lest I forget, very wealthy." Her breath hitched in her throat. "By the way, did you freaking taste that champagne on the flight over here? And in a private jet, nonetheless." She fanned herself.

"The point?"

"Right. The point is that Slash is in a rarified class of his own. He's the kind of man who craves adventure, seeks out the unusual, and needs a *lot* of variety. For someone like you, he'd be exhausting. I just don't want to see you get hurt, honey. You're my best friend and I love you. I know you like Slash and that's okay. Liking is okay. Having wild monkey sex on a balcony in Italy under the moonlight…" She fanned herself again.

"Oh, God. Anyway, what I'm trying to say is that Slash is not the man for you."

"But he said I made him happy."

Basia let out a deep breath. "Men say things, sometimes *anything*, to get women to sleep with them. I'm sure he's fond of you. No question about that. But he may see you as little more than a challenge. A puzzle to decode. Once that puzzle is decoded, it's over. Just like that. Are you following me? Do you really think Slash is in for the long haul?"

"What's the long haul?"

Basia shook me by the shoulders, the left one still tingling from where Slash's whiskers had brushed against my skin. "Listen to me, Lexi. Do you even know Slash's real name?"

I shook my head.

"My point, exactly. You aren't going to ever be able to have him in the way you want."

"Technically, I don't know *what* I want although I'm starting to form a pretty decent hypothesis."

She rolled her eyes. "I'm just saying, be careful around Slash. He's a difficult temptation to resist, but you don't want to be ruined. You have an open heart. Trust me. Stick with Finn. A hook up with Slash would only hurt you down the line. A lot."

"I don't know. It was feeling pretty good to me."

She didn't say anything else and I let it drop because I didn't feel like arguing any more. My brain had semi-returned and I was beginning to think logically again. Unfortunately, Basia was making sense. It probably was a good thing she'd come out on the balcony when she did.

What if kissing *had* led to monkey sex, whatever the heck that was? What if someone else had seen us, like Tito or Elvis or Xavier? Now that I thought about it, my cheeks got hot. What the heck was I thinking? Oh yeah, that *was* the problem. I wasn't freaking thinking, whatsoever.

I followed Basia back to the suite. At least Slash had been right about one thing. Whether we wanted to or not, we needed to get some sleep. We had no idea what we'd find at the cemetery tomorrow and our brains needed to be fresh and ready for anything—dead or alive.

Chapter Twelve

The drive to Vaprio d'Adda took just over six hours. Slash's sedan was large for a car in Italy, but with six of us, it was a tight squeeze. Basia volunteered to sit in the middle of the front seat between Slash and Tito. It didn't escape my notice that it prevented Slash and I from sitting in close proximity. Not that there was anything planned with a full crowd of people. Still, I squeezed in the back between the twins.

I was kept from being too cranky by the fact that Slash, Elvis, Xavier and I had successfully hacked into Rutgon's accounts earlier in the morning. Between the four of us, we discovered six accounts scattered across the world. Two of them had recent deposits of nine million euros. Can anyone say 'bingo?'

In the meantime, Basia and Tito had compiled everything they could find on Francesco Melzi, his background, paintings, painting techniques, and connection to Leonardo da Vinci. Since we were headed to the city where he was most famous, it made sense to accumulate what knowledge we could. Tito told us about the speculation that da Vinci and Melzi were lovers and that was why Melzi had been named executor of his estate. What, if anything, that had to do with the painting and why we were headed to Vaprio d'Adda, we didn't know.

We still didn't understand how it all played out with Maisto either. Tito reported they were at the cutting edge of pharmaceutical medical research with several major research studies underway for a couple of promising drugs to help patients with Multiple Sclerosis, Duchenne Muscular Dystrophy and Parkinson's Disease. They seemed legit and we didn't have a clue why or how they'd be mixed up with a guy like Rutgon.

For now.

We stopped twice during our trip. Once for a bathroom break and once for dinner to go. Slash conducted some evasive maneuvers to make sure we weren't being followed, but I didn't see how it was possible to know if we were or not. When we finally arrived at the small cemetery, it was almost dark. We parked in the empty parking lot. Tito and Slash unpacked our gear and we each got a flashlight and turned it on. We had all dressed in the oldest clothes we had with us. I'd worn a light windbreaker and the jeans I had on when the perfume disaster had occurred at Nonna's. I wished I hadn't, because I'd smelled up the car for the whole trip. I'd also discovered the perfume bottle was still in my pocket. My worst fear was someone would sit on my lap or drop something heavy on me and then we'd all have to suffer anew. I thought about dumping it in the trash at one of our stops, but what if Nonna asked for it back?

Thankfully, everyone was too polite to keep mentioning the smell after the first round of gagging, but I wished I'd thought to rinse my pants in the hotel sink or send them to the hotel valet for washing.

Elvis had the GPS into which he'd entered the exact coordinates from the painting, so we let him lead the way. We passed through an ancient cast iron gate and onto a rocky dirt path. I was kind of sorry we weren't seeing the cemetery in the day, because it looked fascinating. Night had fallen quickly, but the light of the nearly full moon helped illuminate the area and cast a luminescent glow over the headstones. They gave off an eerie glint as we passed. Basia drew in a breath more than once before moving closer to Xavier as we walked by a pair of fierce stone creatures standing sentinel at a tomb. A few steps later, another headstone caught my eye because of its unusual shape and size. I paused and shined my flashlight beam over it.

"Jeez. Is that supposed to be an angel or a gargoyle?"

Tito stepped up beside me and tried to read the headstone. It was largely illegible. "I suppose it would depend on who's buried here, yah? It's too old. I can't read the inscription."

Xavier looked over my shoulder. "Acid weathering will render it unreadable. However, if it's intended to be a celestial being, it's not a very peaceful representation of heavenly pursuits."

"No kidding."

We continued on, passing graves with enormous stone crosses and strange-looking obelisks. Elvis spoke.

"'*There the traveller meets aghast,*
Sheeted Memories of the past—
Shrouded forms that start and sigh,
As they pass the wanderer by—
White-robed forms of friends long given,
In agony to Earth—and Heaven.'"

"Dude." I was impressed. "Edgar Allen Poe?"

"Yes. His poem Dreamland."

We went a few more yards when Elvis abruptly stopped near a large raised sarcophagus as the GPS beeped.

"X marks the spot, team."

Two stone angels leaned over the sarcophagus on either side, appearing to guard it.

"Who's buried here?" I asked.

Slash held a small battery-operated lantern close to the headstone. "It says Volante Melzi, 1475-1523."

Basia stepped up next to me. "That would be Francesco Melzi's mother."

Slash knelt next by the headstone. "Interesting. When was Melzi born?"

"1491."

"The dates would fit. She would have borne him when she was sixteen."

"There are empty spaces on the tomb, but no other names," I observed.

"*Si.* A family crypt but only one member of the family buried here. Odd. Basia, was there any mention of Melzi's father or any siblings?"

"None. Not a single mention of either."

Tito leaned against the sarcophagus. "I wonder why the mom wasn't buried with her son. Isn't his tomb a few kilometers away?"

Basia peered at one of the angels. "Yes. He's buried on his estate."

"Well, maybe he and his mom didn't get along." I shrugged. "It's not so farfetched. He left Mom here and got his own tomb in which he encased himself and his own immediate family."

"I still think it's odd." Slash straightened. "Let's take a closer look at this crypt."

We shone our flashlights over the structure. Behind the sarcophagus was a marble wall flanked by two Romanesque columns that held up a small triangular stone roof. A stone cherub sat at the foot of one of the pillars, gazing up at a small alcove built into the wall. There were deep nicks in the wall and some writing that was nearly illegible.

"Over here," I said, pointing to the alcove. "There's something written here in Italian, I think."

Basia read the words aloud and then translated. "*Tutte le nostre conoscenze ha le sue origini nella nostra percezione.* All our knowledge has its origins in our perceptions."

Slash came and stood next to me. "Leonardo da Vinci."

I nodded. "Yes. It makes sense. They were friends, teacher and pupil, lovers or whatever."

Basia linked her arm with mine. "Well, they were close enough that Da Vinci made Melzi the executor of his considerable estate."

Tito tapped on the inscription. "So, is the quote significant to what we're looking for?"

"Technically, we don't know *what* we're looking for." I wound my ponytail around my finger in a nervous gesture. "We're looking for a clue. Something that has to do with the painting. I think."

Slash strode over to the sarcophagus, patted the lid. "We need to get a look inside."

Basia took a step back. "God, I *knew* you were going to say that."

Tito tried to push the lid but it didn't budge.

I shined my flashlight along the seam. "It's a solid piece of stone. It's not two pieces as in lid and bottom. It's all one piece. There is no way to open it."

Xavier frowned. "That can't be good."

Both Tito and Slash independently inspected the lid, finally concurring with me.

Slash shoved his hand through his hair. "There has to be an opening somewhere."

Basia looked relieved. "Maybe this tomb was intended for one person. Put her in, seal her up, end of story. No opening needed. Ever."

Slash wasn't buying it. He strode over to the cherub statue. "This is located in an odd spot. Perhaps it is a catalyst of some kind." He pressed against the statue starting with the head and working his way down.

Elvis got on his hands and knees and started crawling along the base of the sarcophagus, shining his flashlight along the spot where the stone met the ground. Xavier, Basia and Tito began examining the crypt wall inch by inch for any kind of clue.

There was nothing else for me to look at, so I climbed on top of the sarcophagus and began shining my flashlight along the lid, feeling every crevice with my fingers. It was a big sarcophagus and the going was slow and painstaking. After several minutes, Tito came to stand beside me.

"How's it going, Lexi?" He put a hand on the cold stone. "Need some help?"

I didn't have a chance to answer because Elvis yelled, "I found something."

Suddenly the night was split by the sound of rock grinding against rock and a thudding snap. The sarcophagus wobbled beneath me and then opened. I started to fall, so I screamed and reached out at the thing nearest to me… Tito. My fingers closed around his thick T-shirt and a sickening rip sounded as I fell a good three meters and landed on watery ground right on my butt with a jarring thump. I still held Tito's ripped shirt in my hand.

"*Lexi!*"

Everyone started shouting, but it took me a minute to catch the breath that had been knocked out of me. "Relax. I'm okay."

I wiggled my extremities and nothing appeared broken, however my rump was sore. I immediately shoved my hand into my pocket to find with relief that the perfume Nonna had given me was also still intact. Thank God. I could manage a sore bum, but not if I reeked like a field of white gardenias.

I rubbed my rear as I looked up into the shining light at the top of the hole. "What happened?"

Basia's face appeared. "Elvis found a switch or something. It opened a trap door on top of the sarcophagus right where you were sitting."

"Jeez. Tell Tito I'm sorry. I have his shirt. Unfortunately, it's a complete loss."

"It's okay. Actually, he's excellent eye-candy without a shirt on, but it is a little chilly. We explained to him that you have this habit of stripping clothes off men."

"*What?*" Heat crept up the back of my neck. "I do not."

"Do too." She laughed. "Just ask Elvis."

I was glad it was dark so no one could see my red face as I remembered my first awkward encounter with Elvis at the beach. "Just throw me down a flashlight. I must have dropped mine."

A flashlight came hurtling down and landed with a wet thud a few feet away. I picked it up and to my relief it turned on. Its yellow glow shone feebly in the light.

"See anything?" Elvis called down.

I swept the beam around. "Thankfully I don't see Melzi's mother. At least not yet, anyway." I wasn't necessarily squeamish, but being surrounded by bones or skeletons in the dark might freak me out.

"It's also pretty damp down here. Okay, so someone explain this to me. If that opening is the entrance to the crypt, how did they get the bones or a coffin down here?"

Tito answered. "They must have lowered it down with something. Ropes probably."

"You'd think they'd build some stairs."

Basia snorted. "What would be the purpose? Lower the body into the crypt. Close it up. Forever. If you go in there, you're not coming out."

"Good point, which begs the question, 'Why is there a tunnel here?'" I stepped closer to the opening, swinging the beam of my flashlight around it.

"There's a tunnel?" Slash's voice sounded excited.

"Yeah, but it's small. Crawl-worthy only. Hands-and-knees height. I'll check it out."

"You will not, *cara*. Not without me." In seconds Slash appeared in the entrance with a rope tied around his waist. He instructed Tito to hold it and he slid down. He untied the rope and tugged it once. It slithered back up to the top and disappeared.

Slash came over to me, pulled me into his chest. "You took ten years off my life, disappearing into the sarcophagus like that."

"I assure you, it was unplanned."

He cupped my cheek with his hand and I thought he was going to kiss me when Elvis appeared at the opening.

"I'm going, too." He began tying the rope around his waist.

Xavier protested. "Dude, you're claustrophobic."

"Not anymore."

Slash released me and began examining the tunnel by the beam of his flashlight.

A minute later Elvis landed in the crypt, his shoes sucking into the muddy ground as he took a step toward me. "You sure you okay, Lexi? I feel responsible. I had no idea the switch would open a trapdoor on top of the sarcophagus."

"Of course, you didn't."

"Nothing broken?"

"Nope. Just shook up. Literally and figuratively."

Slash straightened, calling up to the others. "Lower down the lantern. The rest of you stay there until we know what's going on. Or if we don't come back."

I glanced at Slash, not liking how that sounded. I hoped he was kidding, but his face was shrouded in the shadows.

Tito appeared at the entrance. "Agreed. I'll be needed to pull you all up." He lowered the lantern and Elvis got it.

"Be careful, Lexi." Basia peered into the hole. "You're crawling around in a crypt, for God's sake."

"Gee, thanks for the gruesome reminder, Basia. Sure you don't want to come?"

Slash knelt on his hands and knees at the tunnel entrance. "The fewer people in here, the better. Let's go take a look at what we've got."

Just like that, he and his light disappeared into the tunnel. Elvis motioned to me to go next, so I took a deep breath and followed.

Chapter Thirteen

I'm not claustrophobic like Elvis, but I'll admit I did not like crawling around in a crypt tunnel, especially when I had no idea where I was headed. There was some comfort in the fact that I had two guys on either side of me, ready to pull me in one direction or the other, if things got hairy. Also, I was eternally thankful that Slash went first, most likely destroying any spider webs or scaring away any potentially crawly creatures that would be in the way. I tried not to think about it.

The tunnel was small and it was a good thing none of us had a lot of fat on us, because that would have been significantly problematic. The tunnel itself was dry, but the mold and musty smell was strong. I breathed through my mouth, trying to calm my racing heart and pretending that I was on a grand adventure that didn't involve potential dead bodies, ghosts, or assorted creepy bugs. I could hear both Slash and Elvis breathing hard. The cacophony of sound somehow comforted me. I'm sure I would have freaked out within minutes if I'd been crawling around alone.

After what seemed like an eternity, Slash muttered an oath and then he called back that there was a small drop-off ahead. I carefully crawled a few feet more and saw Slash's hand extending to me. I took it and he pulled me out of the tunnel and into a small cavern. I stood, my knees aching from the crawl. My ponytail was plastered to the back of my neck and I realized I'd been sweating. I couldn't tell if it were from fear or exertion. Moments later, Slash pulled Elvis out of the tunnel. His face was deathly pale and I imagined crawling in the tunnel and keeping a handle on his claustrophobia had taken its toll on him. I wished I could do something to help, but here we were, stuck in claustrophobic hell.

I glanced around. "Where are we?"

Slash held up the lantern. We stood in a cavern approximately ten meters high and six meters wide. There was no discernible exit. More importantly, it had no body, coffin, urn or evidence that Melzi's mother had been buried here.

I rubbed my nose with the back of my hand. "Jeez. This is just weird."

"There has to be access to the outside." Elvis shined his flashlight across the rock ceiling. "A small access hole, at the least. There is air in here. But it will be impossible to detect the source at night."

I scanned the ceiling with my flashlight beam, too, but Elvis was right. It would be impossible to pinpoint the source without light.

Slash was examining the walls with the light of the lantern. "There's writing over here, too."

I stood next to him, adding my beam to his. "It looks like hieroglyphics."

Elvis stood on the other side of Slash. "Egyptian, by the looks of it."

I frowned. "Why in the world would there be ancient Egyptian hieroglyphics in an Italian crypt?"

Slash ran his fingers over the drawings. "This is not

ancient. But it is old. I suspect it was drawn at the same time the crypt was constructed. It must be significant."

I leaned closer to peer at the markings. "In what way? A message of some kind?"

"*Si.* Or a warning."

A shiver ran up my spine. "But for whom?"

"Perhaps, *cara.* But I have a feeling it wouldn't have been so easy."

Sighing, I took a deep breath and began studying the image. I had to clear my mind and try to understand the significance of why someone had drawn Egyptian hieroglyphics in an empty cavern off the maternal crypt of one of Italy's minor artists. Jeez. For all I could tell, she wasn't even buried here. Could this situation get any more bizarre?

Still, it could be worse. We could deal with hieroglyphics. After all, hieroglyphics were a code of sorts, and all three of us in this cave were pretty good at cracking code.

Elvis's breathing seemed less harsh and I realized having something to focus on had eased his claustrophobia. He leaned his forearm against the wall. "Here's my initial take. I think this figure is a king. He's holding a staff of sorts and it looks like he may be wearing a crown."

I squinted. "You mean that blob on his head?"

"Yes."

It didn't look much like a crown to me and I wasn't even sure the figure was male, but I went with it. "Well, if he's a king, it looks like he's being offered something on a platter. See that triangle-looking thing on a plate? I think it's a plate. What do you think? Is it food or a gift?"

Elvis traced the shape with his fingertip. "Food. In

Egypt, only royalty or the gods were offered the conical loaf."

Slash leaned his head against the wall and closed his eyes. Was he thinking or taking a nap? It was hard to tell.

I turned my attention back to the etchings. "The conical loaf. It rings a vague bell."

Elvis nodded. "Probably, and not just in terms of food. The ancient Egyptians were guided by the *Shem-an-na*, the Book of the Dead. The conical loaf was referred to as a mixture bread and powdered gold and offered to kings or the gods in an elaborate ceremony."

"Wow. That would be expensive bread."

"I suppose if it's an offering fit for king or god, that's the idea."

"So, was it presumed that adding the powered gold gave it some sort of mystical powers?"

"Supposedly."

Slash spoke up. "Actually the powered gold did provide a medicinal aspect, which may account for the belief that the conical load held mystical powers." He'd opened his eyes and was looking at the hieroglyphics again. "The theory is known as chi and prana."

Elvis nodded, his voice excited. "Yes. That's it. Chi and prana. In the spiritual world they are considered substances made of energy that can enter the body via special breathing techniques."

"*Si*. There may be a connection. Chi and prana must be derived from a precious metal element and be able to be ground into a powder, as well as exist in either oil or vapor form. The conical loaf would qualify."

It took me a minute, but I began to understand what they were talking about. "Wait, that sounds like a transition element in chemistry."

"*Si.*"

I pondered a moment. "Okay, then that means a chi or prana substance must be able to transit from metallic to either a diatomic or monatomic state through a chemical reaction."

Elvis tapped the loaf with his finger. "Exactly, which is why I presume Slash mentioned the medicinal aspect."

A light bulb dinged in my head. "Okay, I've got a thought. Chi and prana. Transition chemistry. Arcane chemistry. Essentially we're talking alchemy here, right?"

Both Elvis and Slash looked at me, startled. The beams from the flashlights caused the light to dance in eerie shadows across their faces.

I raised my hands. "I don't know why or how alchemy would fit in with Egyptian hieroglyphics carved into a wall at the end of an underground tunnel in a crypt in a small Italian town. Just thought I'd throw it out there."

Slash turned and began running the light over the edge of the cave. "Good, *cara.* Very good. We need to examine every inch of this room."

Elvis and I exchanged a puzzled glance.

"Okay, dude. What are we looking for?" Elvis asked.

"A formula, a numerical sequence, more writings. There has to be something to relate to chi and prana in this cave."

I thought about the others waiting for us at the graveside. "I think someone should report to Tito and the others."

"Better yet, bring them." Slash pointed at me. "Except for Tito. We need him as our anchor."

"Will we all fit in here?"

"It will be a tight squeeze, but we could use the extra set of eyes. Additional brainpower never hurt, either."

Remembering how claustrophobic Elvis was, I turned to him. "You want to go get them?" It was basically just exchanging one tight space for another, but he might want, or need, a change of scenery.

He shot me a grateful look. "Sure. Thanks."

He disappeared back into the tunnel as I walked three steps to the other side of the cave and started a painstaking search of the walls. It was hard work in such poor light. My fingers brushed against the stone just in case I would feel something my eyes might miss in the dim light of my flashlight.

Several minutes later I could hear Basia and Xavier making their way through the tunnel. Basia was complaining about her fingernails and Xavier was commenting on how ace crawling around a crypt could be.

Moments later they popped out of the tunnel.

Basia held her nose. "Oh, my God. It smells awful in here."

Sighing, I took the perfume bottle out of my pocket and sprayed it around a bit. "There. Better?"

Basia took a sniff and then gagged. "Worse. Where did you get that awful perfume?"

I pocketed it. "Careful. It was a present."

Elvis showed them the hieroglyphics and quickly brought them up to speed on our thoughts. "So, Slash thinks there has to be another clue here somewhere."

Xavier whistled. "Related to chi and prana? It's like another needle in a haystack."

Basia sighed. "Does everything connected to you people have to be so cryptic? For once, can't the answer just be right in front of us?"

We all just looked at her, so with a harrumph, she turned her back and started examining the walls.

Slowly and carefully, we made our way around the

cave. The space was quiet except for our breathing, the shuffling of our feet, and the occasional scrape of our fingernails across the stone. After what had surely been an hour or more, my eyes were aching, my neck had a crick, and my fingers were sore from gripping the flashlight. I stepped back to take a break while Basia kept complaining.

"This is nuts. Certifiable, in fact. Doesn't anyone else see the weirdness of all of this? I'm feeling up the walls of a freaking crypt, for pity's sake. This is *not* normal."

I let out a breath, brushed my hand against my forehead, and leaned back against the wall. I understood her frustration and she did have a point.

Basia turned around, slid down the wall to the ground. "Ouch! Ouch!" She leaped up almost immediately, clutching her butt. "Crap. That hurt."

My irritation rose. "Oh, don't be such a baby, Basia. It's just a few rocks."

Basia snarled. "Don't you *dare* call me a baby. Not after I followed you into this hellhole." She beamed her light on the floor. "And this is not just a *few* rocks. It's a pointy pyramid rock. You'd say ouch, too, if you had this poke your ass."

Everyone in the cave stilled. After a moment, Basia looked at us alarmed, her flashlight going from face to face. "What? What's *wrong* with you people?"

We all pounced on her at the same time, pretty much knocking her out of the way.

Slash knelt at the rock first, studying its formation in the beam of his flashlight. "Definitely conical-shaped."

I knelt beside him. "I don't see any markings on it."

Slash began making a dirt trench around the base of the rock with his fingertips. "It's not natural. It's manmade."

Elvis looked over my shoulder. "Agreed. It's too symmetrical to be natural. There has to be something here."

I ran my fingers down along the base of the rock where Slash methodically pulled the dirt away. On the side farthest from me, I felt an irregular bump.

"I've got something." I tapped on the spot and Slash aimed the lantern at the spot.

Slash finger landed on top of mine and I slid mine away so he could feel it. "*Si*, you've found something, *cara*."

Slash turned himself on his side, and half-slid, half-wedged himself between the cone-shaped rock and the wall of the cave to get a better look. "It looks like it has a hinge of some kind."

Since there was no way none of us could squeeze back there to confirm it, we took Slash's word for it.

I put my hand on top the rock. "Which way is the hinge set?"

"It looks like it should open to the left." Slash pulled on it. "But the hinge isn't budging and I don't want to pull too hard in case I break it."

I glanced up at Elvis. "We need a natural lubricant."

Elvis nodded and without a word, he and Xavier began crawling about the floor.

Basia, apparently forgetting all about her sore bottom, stood by watching us work. "What did I find?"

I shook my head. "I don't know, but there seems to be a conical theme going on here. There might be something hidden beneath or inside this rock. We're just following the clues and see where they take us."

Elvis came back holding a slug. A thin trail of slime hung from its body. "Best I can do on short notice."

Basia took a step back. "Gross."

Slash took the slug. "It may not be enough. But let's give it a shot."

He pinched the slime between his fingers rubbing it on the hinge. He repeated the action a few more times and then carefully set the slug down. Call me sappy, but I was glad he didn't hurt the little guy.

After a moment, Slash tried pulling the rock again, but nothing happened. He swore softly. "I'm going to need more lubricant."

Xavier brought over what looked like a dripping fungus. "Try this."

Slash took it without comment and rubbed it onto the hinge. After a moment, he pulled at the rock again. This time we all heard something give. The cave filled with the sound of a grinding, screeching noise, and it wasn't coming from the pyramid rock. In the small confines of the cave, it sounded abnormally loud.

Xavier swung his beam around the cave trying to pinpoint the source. "Whatever you just did, dude, it's working."

I tried to determine the source of the sound, but the echo factor inside the cave killed any possibility of determining where it was located.

"What's going on?" Basia stood close to Xavier, linking her arms with him.

"I'm not sure."

"Over here." Elvis shouted over the grinding noise. By the light of his beam, we saw a rock rolling aside, revealing a partial opening to another tunnel.

"Sweet." Xavier pumped his fist in the air.

"Oh, God, no." Basia moaned. "Not another tunnel. Can't we just find diamonds and go home?"

Slash knelt at the opening, illuminating the entrance with his lantern beam. "I don't think it's a long tunnel.

I smell fresh air. We've got to push this rock the rest of the way open."

Only one more person could fit in the space next to Slash. Although I was sure I was physically stronger than either of the twins, I didn't want to put a mark on their man cards. So I stayed back as Xavier stepped forward and the two of them began to push, grunting and straining to get it open. After a few minutes Elvis replaced Xavier and the pushing continued. I was about to volunteer to help when the rock suddenly rolled the rest of the way.

"Ace," breathed Xavier.

Slash crawled in without hesitation and Elvis right behind him. I followed Elvis and heard the others clamber in behind me. Slash had been right. The tunnel was short. I crawled out and into a large labyrinth of underground catacombs.

"Holy necropolis, Batman." I looked around in wonder. "I don't think we're in Gotham City anymore."

The labyrinth contained four separate tunnels. In the first two tunnels to the right, I could see two skeletons, one in a top stone bunk and the other in the lower bunk, both carved into the wall.

Basia stood beside me and gasped. "I didn't read anything about catacombs in Vaprio d'Adda."

"I knew nothing, as well." Slash strode to the point at which the tunnels forked.

I had no idea how far the catacombs stretched. "Could this be connected to Melzi's tomb?"

"Unlikely." Slash shined his light on the skeletons. "I don't see any markings here, but one of these skeletons is a woman. The other is a child. Six, maybe seven years old."

"Melzi's mother?"

Slash shrugged. "Hard to say."

Elvis called out from one of the other tunnels. "I checked these two far tunnels. These are empty berths and I don't see any more bones."

"None in this one either," Xavier added.

While the discovery was exciting, even monumental, I was about ready to get the heck out from underground. Dead bodies gave me the heebie jeebies. "Is there another exit?"

Elvis pointed up. "There's a draft in here. There must be some kind of opening to the ground above."

The ceiling of the labyrinth was high and dark. I could see no visible way to climb up.

"Might this be significant?" Basia pointed to something on one side of the wall.

I walked over to her. "It's writing. Italian, right?"

Basia nodded. "It says *'A mother's love for her child is the key.'*"

"So, maybe it is Melzi's mother. I wonder who the child is?"

Slash came to stand beside me. "A mother's love." He started to pace and then abruptly turned toward the two skeletons.

I gasped when he started lifting the bones of the one on the top. He set them carefully on the floor one by one.

I stared open-mouthed at him. "Slash, doesn't the word desecration mean anything to you?"

"Dude." Even Elvis seemed appalled.

Slash ignored us. When all the bones were on the floor, he felt beneath the slab. After a moment, he held up a key. "Anyone see a treasure chest?"

My mouth dropped open. "No freaking way."

"Way."

I rubbed my forehead. "Although I'm impressed, I'm also a bit grossed out. You were just handling human remains."

Slash rolled his eyes. "Spread out and see if you can find anything a key will open."

"There might be a door this way." Elvis pointed at the third tunnel. "I thought it an alcove, but upon seeing that key, it may merit a closer look."

Slash picked up the lantern and walked down the third tunnel with the rest of us following behind. Elvis pointed to the alcove, which was set back into the wall to the right of the tunnel. Slash raised the lantern to examine it closer.

"Here." Slash pointed to a keyhole and began brushing dirt and debris from the opening.

There was a faint beeping noise and Xavier tapped on his watch. "I'd better go back to update Tito soon."

Before anyone could answer we heard a shuffling noise in the labyrinth behind us. Alarmed, we hurried back into the large cavern just in time to see Tito crawling out of the tunnel, wearing Slash's jacket. It was half-unzipped and I could see the cross around his neck and his chest hair peeking out. I cringed, thinking of the ripped remains of his shirt I'd left on the crypt floor.

I got there first. "Hey, Tito. Why aren't you waiting for us?"

He stood and lifted his arms as someone else crawled out of the tunnel directly behind him, pressing a gun into his back.

Tito's expression was grim. "Sorry, guys. We've got company."

Chapter Fourteen

"Bianca."

Slash's angry voice echoed through the labyrinth. He had his gun in his hand and pointed it at her. She was dressed in a black spandex jumpsuit, a dark jacket and combat boots, her long dark hair pulled back into a braid. Her eyes were cold and mean as she surveyed the room. She kept her gun pressed into Tito's back other until another guy crawled out of the tunnel behind her. He was dressed in black fatigues, boots and wore a large rifle strapped on a belt around his shoulder and torso. He wore a special headband with a light and had a gun in his hand, too.

"James Rutgon!" It slipped out of my mouth before I could stop it.

He'd cut his hair military-style, but I recognized his face. Unfortunately, as soon as I said his name, he pointed his gun at me.

"Lexi Carmichael?"

I clamped my mouth shut. Without looking at Slash, Rutgon said, "Drop the gun, dude, or I waste her this second."

"Angelico." Bianca lifted the gun from the small of Tito's back and pushed him forward. She pointed her gun at Slash. "Do as he says. He'll kill her and then I'll kill you."

Slash narrowed his eyes. "I'll kill him first."

Bianca shrugged. "Maybe. But she'll die, too, so this discussion is pointless. We both know you aren't going to let him kill her."

Rutgon released the safety and the click echoed in the cave. His eyes were hard and purposeful. I was serious toast.

Basia started to cry. "Oh, God, Slash. He'll shoot her. Put it down."

Rutgon didn't take his gaze off me.

Bianca spoke. "*Uno.*"

I closed my eyes.

"*Due.*"

My stomach heaved. Oh, jeez. I was going to throw up right before I got shot. Could I not die with dignity? The irony of this situation was not lost on me. I never imagined my demise would conveniently occur in a crypt where no one would even have to freaking bury me. No funeral, no wailing, no gnashing of the teeth. Just bye-bye, Lexi. The end.

I tensed, waiting for the gunshot, the searing pain and then the nothingness.

There was a long pause and silence. I cracked open my eyes and saw Slash lowering his arm and putting the gun on the floor. He slid it toward Rutgon.

Bianca smiled at him. "Wise decision, Angelico."

Slash didn't answer. My breath whooshed out of me in a rush. I hadn't even realized I was holding it.

Rutgon pointed at Basia. "You, girl. Get the gun."

Basia pointed at her chest. She was shaking. "Me? I don't know how to handle a gun."

"Shut up. Just pick it up and hand it to me, handle first. If you try anything, I'll kill you. Do it."

"Oh, God." Trembling, Basia walked two steps, gingerly picked up the gun with two fingers and gave it to Rutgon with the handle out. He pocketed it.

Bianca said something else to Slash in Italian. He bent down and pulled a knife out of his boot, sliding it across the floor. He then pulled another gun from the back of his waist and put that on the floor as well.

Rutgon lowered his gun and circled behind Slash, barking an order in Italian to him. Slash slowly put his hands behind his back and Rutgon snapped some cuffs on his hands. Then Rutgon patted Slash down with military precision and then forced him to sit against the wall. Tito was the next to get cuffed. Since he didn't get the pat down, I assumed he'd already been searched for weapons.

Rutgon did a cursory examination of the rest of us, relieving us of our flashlights, not bothering to cuff the twins or Basia and I. Guess we didn't look like serious threats.

When Rutgon got to me, he put his face inches from mine and smirked. "So, you are the famous Lexi Carmichael."

I lifted an eyebrow. "I'm famous?"

"In certain circles." He glanced over at the twins. "So are they. I can't believe I'm meeting you guys at the same time. Although you and I could have met a little earlier if I'd been quicker with the umbrella."

"That was you?"

"Didn't recognize me? We could share some cool stories, you know."

I shrugged. "I doubt it. You're not in our league."

He blinked in surprise. "What did you say?"

"I'm pretty sure there's nothing wrong with your hearing."

His face turned red. "You can't talk to me like that. I hacked into the Vatican Bank." The back of his hand caught my right-side jaw and lip.

Everyone started yelling and Slash struggled to get to his feet. Bianca shouted for us to freeze and then said something angrily to Rutgon in Italian. He didn't answer. His focus and fury was on me alone.

I straightened, meeting Rutgon's eyes. "You didn't hack, James. You planted a gateway program. I could have done that in the first grade. You're a wanna-be hacker. Sorry, dude, you can hit me again, but that's a fact."

I braced myself for another hit, but Bianca snapped something at him. He ground his teeth and began to pat me down, a bit roughly. I glanced over at Slash and he gave me a warning shake of his head.

Rutgon found the lump in my front right jean's pocket and pulled out the small bottle of perfume. He examined and then sniffed it with disbelief. He coughed twice.

"What's this?"

"Perfume. It was a present."

He wrinkled his nose and shoved it back at me. "Spray some on yourself."

"What?"

"I want to make sure it's perfume. Spray it on."

I popped up the lid and sprayed as little as I could on my wrist. In seconds the entire cave reeked like Nonna's perfume.

Rutgon held his nose. "Jesus, someone must really hate you to give you that as a present. Put it away."

I stuffed it in my pocket and took a step back.

Rutgon glanced over at Bianca. "Let's get what we came for and get out of here."

Slash tipped his head toward Rutgon. "Why are you in league with him, Bianca?" He spoke in English, probably on purpose, to give us a better idea of what was going on.

She ignored him.

I could see Slash flexing his wrists and hands behind his back while he spoke. "Have you no shame? To betray your country over ideals is bad enough, but for money and with the likes of dirt like him? I thought you knew better."

"Shut up," Rutgon snapped.

Bianca laughed. "Angelico, you don't know anything about this situation."

"*Si*, but I do, Bianca. You're not working for SIMSI. You're working for Maisto."

The look of surprise on her face was enough to confirm that Slash had hit it on the head. Bianca was working for Maisto. But why?

Bianca turned her back on Slash and crooked her finger at me. "Come here, geek girl."

Uh, oh. I approached her, wondering why in the world Slash had ever dated her. Could anyone say complete and utter sociopath?

Her dark eyes bored into mine. "What have you found so far in this cave? Don't lie to me. I will know."

I exchanged a quick glance with Slash, but his face remained impassive. Her hit came out of nowhere, catching me just above the left ear. I staggered to the side and heard a cacophony of yelling. Or it could have been the ringing in my ear.

I pressed my hand to my ear, glaring at Bianca. I was getting tired of being knocked around. What was this—Punch Lexi Day? Although, if I looked at the bright side, I suppose it was better than *Kill* Lexi Day.

"I didn't say you could look at him, girl. When I speak, you look at me. Answer my question."

I shrugged. "We found a cave. Actually, we found a couple of caves and this one had skeletons. Go figure. We must be in a crypt. Other than that, we were just about to call it a night."

She hit me again and Slash shouted something at her in Italian. My lip swelled and my mouth started bleeding. I felt a nasty headache coming on.

Rutgon took Slash's lantern and disappeared down the path where we'd just been. My heart thumped hard. If I remembered correctly, we'd left the key in the keyhole of the door we'd just found. Well, maybe we'd get lucky and he wouldn't notice.

That hope was dashed when he shouted something excitedly in Italian. A thudding noise followed and then some more shouting. Bianca motioned for Slash and Tito to get up. "Seems you forgot to mention something, girl. Angelico, Tito, you go first."

Slash and Tito stood by pressing their backs against the wall and pushing themselves up. They followed Rutgon and we filed after them with Bianca bringing up the rear with the gun.

Elvis leaned forward. "You okay?"

"Yeah, I'll live. For now."

The stone door we'd been about to open before their untimely arrival, stood slightly ajar, the key still in the hole. Rutgon was already inside. I stepped inside, the musty smell hitting me like a fist to the stomach. While the other caverns appeared to have access to at least limited fresh air, this one clearly had been sealed tight.

Once inside, I tried to ignore the smell and looked

around in wonder. The cave was as large as the one we'd just been in, but the centerpiece completely floored me.

I didn't speak to anyone in particular. "Holy crypt. Is that a glass coffin?"

I'd never seen anything like it. A coffin made entirely of glass sat on an ornate raised stone dais. Even in the dim light, it was clear by the striking majesty and elegance of the structure it had to have been created by the hand of a master artist. Rutgon stood next to it, brushing the dust off.

Elvis whistled. "Melzi's mother?"

"Possibly. But why so well hidden and what's with the glass coffin?"

Bianca filed in, still holding the gun. She gasped in surprise when she saw the coffin and then said something to Rutgon. He turned and frowned at Slash and Tito. He stepped away from the coffin, pushing Slash and Tito against the wall and forcing them back into a sitting position.

Rutgon kicked Slash's boot once he was down. "Any time you try to move, hero, someone over here will get shot. Most likely Lexi."

"Hey, thanks," I said. "That makes me feel special."

Rutgon ignored me, taking a third set of handcuffs from his jacket and shackling Slash's ankle to Tito's. He straightened and turned to Bianca. "Okay, now what?"

Bianca considered for a moment and then pointed at me. "Go open the coffin, girl."

I held up my hand. "Not that we're into social niceties and all, but I do have a name, you know."

"Go open that coffin or I'll start shooting."

"Well, if you put it like that." Guess she sucked at conversation more than I did. I calculated the potential usefulness of continuing the conversation and antagonizing her, but didn't see a reason to do so. Yet. Besides, deep down, I really wanted to see what was there.

Slash's lantern sat on the floor, so I picked it up and examined the spot on the coffin that Rutgon had already dusted off. The glass was old and leaded in spots, so it was hard to get a good view of what was inside. However, I was certain of one thing.

"There isn't a body in here. At least not a skeleton."

"Ashes?" The question came from Elvis.

I peered into the coffin again, carefully brushing more dust away. "It's hard to tell in this light and with the quality of the glass. But why put ashes in a coffin? Why not an urn?"

"Do you see anything else?" Bianca spoke. "A scroll or writings of some kind?"

I turned around to face her. "You expecting something?"

"Just look."

I turned back around, carefully dusting off a wider area. In the middle of the coffin, I spied what looked to be a small blob. "Well, there's definitely something in here. But what I don't know."

Bianca said something to Rutgon and he joined me at the coffin. He frowned when I pointed to the dark spot. "There. The light is blocked. There's something there."

Bianca couldn't hide her excitement. "Give it to me."

Slash said something in an angry stream of Italian. Bianca snarled something at him. Rutgon suddenly grabbed me, pushing the gun into the side of my neck. My breath froze as he increased the pressure of the cold steel against my skin.

Bianca's voice was chilly, controlled. "I told Angelico that if he speaks again, I'll kill you. I don't care if the coffin is booby-trapped. I've got plenty of volunteers here. Either open the coffin or die."

Rutgon released me, pushing me hard toward the coffin. I stumbled, but caught myself. I looked over my shoulder as he took several steps back.

"Wait." Elvis held up a hand. "Let me do it. I took a year of historical archeology. Whatever is in there, I'll need to be careful with it so I don't destroy it before we can see what it is."

Bianca thought for a moment. "Okay. You can help her."

"I'd rather do it myself."

"I don't care what you want. Help her or shut up."

Elvis joined me at the dais. I'd never been so grateful to have someone at my side. "Okay, what next?" I asked him.

He took the lantern from me, examining the lip of the lid. He ran his finger along the crease. "The coffin is sealed."

I knelt beside him. "With what?"

"Wax, I think."

He rubbed his finger and thumb together, then smelled it. "A heavy protective wax. Smart. It will have sealed out moisture and air, perfectly preserving whatever is inside."

I walked around the coffin, running my finger along the seam. "It's sealed around the entire lid."

"We'll need something sharp to open it."

I looked over at Bianca. "We need Slash's knife. We can't open the lid without it. It's sealed."

She considered. "Okay. But if you try anything…" She strode over to Basia and pressed the gun against her temple. Basia didn't make a sound, but her face went deathly pale.

I swallowed hard. "I'm not going to try anything."

Bianca nodded and Rutgon got the knife from her and handed it to me. It felt heavy in my hand. I didn't dare look over at Basia. I took the knife and knelt beside the coffin.

"Do you think it's safe?" I asked Elvis.

He shrugged. "Hard to say. Slash could be right. It could be booby-trapped. Or there could be a poisonous gas trapped inside. Or moving the lid could trigger something to happen. Remember in Indiana Jones when he picked up the statue and the boulder was released, almost crushing him? We just don't know."

Bianca snapped at us. "Stop talking and get working."

I turned toward the coffin and whispered, "Idiot."

Elvis smiled as I lifted the knife. "Looks like we don't have much of a choice in what to do."

"No, we don't."

I pressed the knife into the wax and pulled it sideways. A glob came off on the knife, so I wiped it off and continued. Elvis and I took turns all around the coffin. I had no idea how long it took, but my knees, back and arms ached from the effort. When we reached our starting spot, we stood, stretching out our muscles.

"Give me the knife back and try to open it." Bianca waved her gun at me. "Now."

I gave Bianca the knife. Elvis and I pushed at the coffin lid, but it was too heavy and the wax probably still stuck in places. We grunted and pushed for a bit more, but the lid did not move an iota.

"It's too heavy." I panted and wiped at my brow. "We need some help here."

Bianca gestured at Rutgon and he walked over to us, putting the gun in his waistband at the small of his back.

He added his strength and the three of us pushed again. I felt the lid give a little, but not much. After a few more tries, Bianca ordered Basia and Xavier to help. We all took a spot along the coffin and pushed.

After a minute of intense pushing, the lid began to slide. At that exact moment, I heard a noise behind us. From the corner of my eye, Tito and Slash pushed to their feet and in a weird sync, launched themselves at Bianca. Rutgon whirled around and took a step toward them, reaching for his gun, but Elvis neatly tripped him and he sprawled face first onto the cave floor.

In a moment of inspiration, I threw myself on him, clawing for the gun. Elvis and Xavier joined me and we scratched and struggled in a tangle of heads and limbs. Somehow Rutgon disengaged himself from us and came to a crouch, the gun still in his hand. Tito and Slash were using the force of their bodies to knock Bianca into the wall, but without the use of their hands or feet, their effectiveness was limited. Plus Bianca fought like a tiger on PCP.

I screamed a warning as Rutgon whirled and fired the gun. Slash slumped to the floor, taking Tito with him. I stared in horrified shock as Tito tried to get up, but Slash didn't move.

"You bastard." I shrieked, then threw myself at Rutgon, clawing at his face. He pushed me hard and I fell backward into the stone dais, knocking the breath out of me.

In the meantime, Bianca straightened, furious. She kicked Tito hard in the side with her boot over and over, shrieking at him in Italian. Someone else was screaming, possibly me. The cave echoed with a shrieking, ear-splitting symphony. I watched as Tito curled himself up the best he could to protect himself given that his hands were handcuffed behind him and he was chained to Slash, who wasn't moving.

"Bianca, stop it. Stop it. *Stop it*!" I screamed until my voice was hoarse.

She finally looked up at me, breathing hard. Her braid was unraveled and her cheekbone and jaw swelled on one side where the guys had knocked her into the wall. She looked severely shaken and pissed.

She pushed her hair off her face. "That was stupid and careless, Tito. You know what happens to men who don't fall into line with me."

To my horror, she held up her gun and pointed it at him. Before I could open my mouth to say another word, she pulled the trigger. And then, it was too late.

Chapter Fifteen

Tito twitched and lay still. Basia wailed and Xavier pulled her into his arms, holding her tight as she sobbed. I looked up from the floor, frozen in shock and disbelief. The gunshot still rang in my ears.

Slash was down and Bianca had shot Tito. Had the world turned completely upside down?

I struggled for words. "You…you shot him point-blank."

She looked at me with contemptuous eyes. "You doubted I would?"

"He kissed your knuckles."

"*What*?"

Rutgon growled something in Italian. Bianca waved him off. He turned to me, his expression murderous. My nails had raked down both sides of his face and it was bleeding. I felt a vicious sense of satisfaction. He looked like he wanted to shoot me, but Bianca stopped him.

"Not now. We need her." She waved the gun at me. "Get up and finish opening that coffin. Believe me, girl, you are next on my list to die if any of any of you try something stupid like that again."

I had the strangest mixture of emotions. I wanted to execute the perfect karate kick and snap the gun out of Rutgon's hand before shooting him, like he had shot Slash.

I also wanted to curl up and cry, but I looked over at Basia, Xavier and Elvis and knew I had to help them. It took me a few seconds to get my brain functioning, but I got to my feet, keeping a wary eye on Rutgon who still looked like he wanted nothing more in the world than to off me.

My body trembled. My legs were wobbly. My hands were shaking and my teeth chattering. I couldn't even bring myself to look at Slash and Tito. They were probably dead and I wasn't ready to process that yet. My eyes filled with tears, but I took several breaths and tried to compose myself.

Elvis staggered to his feet beside me.

In a surprise move, Rutgon yanked Elvis toward him, wrapping his arm around Elvis's neck in a chokehold. He was still furious and looking for someone to take it out on now that Bianca had told him I was off-limits for the time being.

He hissed in Elvis's ear. "You were an idiot to try to take me on, Zimmerman. I thought you were supposed to be a genius."

He squeezed and Elvis's face started to turn blue.

"God. Stop it. Please." My heart was beating a million thumps a minute and I felt dizzy, sick. Dimly, I could Xavier shouting something, too.

My stomach heaved and I fought down the urge to vomit. "Look, Rutgon, I'm trying to do what you guys want me to do. But I could use Elvis's help and his brainpower in case we run into any trouble. We'll open the coffin and get what's inside. Okay? Just let go of him. I'll have a better chance of doing it if I'm not operating alone. He's got experience. Please. Please, I need him." My final words caught on a sob.

I was falling apart. It was freaking hard to keep it all together when people were getting shot and strangled all around me. As it was, I sucked in normal social situations. Now it was glaringly apparent I behaved even worse in dysfunctional ones.

Elvis started making small choking noises. I knew Rutgon was playing with him, because he could have snapped Elvis's neck in one quick movement. He was enjoying this.

My pleas were falling on deaf ears with Rutgon, so I tried a different approach. "Bianca, think. This coffin might be booby-trapped. I need to figure out how to get past it. Elvis can help me because he has the knowledge. If we fail, we're the ones who will get it first. But if you kill us all off, you'll have to risk your own necks. Calculate the odds, if you don't believe me."

Elvis looked so fragile in Rutgon's arms. After what seemed like an eternity, Bianca finally said something and Rutgon pushed Elvis away with a disgusted grunt. Elvis took a shaky step toward me, rubbing his neck and coughing. I wanted to hug him, but instead offered an arm to steady his legs.

We were both shaking as we climbed the dais together. My brain was so discombobulated that I wondered if I would ever be able to think properly. Slash and Tito were down, probably dead, and we were alone in a crypt with a couple of psychos. For now, I had to concentrate on getting whatever it was out of the coffin and giving it to Bianca. I tried to ignore the part of my brain that was screaming she'd kill us as soon as she had it. If I gave into it I'd be paralyzed and completely useless.

So, for now, I focused on the item in the coffin. The lid was partially askew and I realized that the coffin must not have contained poisonous gases or else we'd all be dead by now. Cautiously I peeked inside the coffin and was surprised to see how pristine the interior had remained.

"The seal worked." Elvis spoke over my shoulder.

I nodded and the two of us pushed the lid farther aside. I could see our prize a bit farther to our left. I leaned over the coffin and stretched out a hand to grab it, but Elvis grabbed my arm, stopping me.

"Wait. Let me do it." In a flash, he pulled off his jersey and wrapped it around his hand.

Rutgon grabbed Elvis by the shoulder. "What are you doing?"

Elvis was naked from the waist up and gooseflesh rose on his arms, chest and neck.

"I'm taking precautions," he said, holding up his hands. "We can't touch a historical and potentially fragile item with our bare hands. Historical archeology 101. So, unless you can lend me a pair of gloves, may I continue?"

Bianca narrowed her eyes but then shrugged. "Let him do it."

As we turned our backs on them and I murmured, "Bull. What's up?"

He murmured in return, "Trust me?"

"Always."

I stepped to the side, so he could access the coffin. He kept his eyes on me as he reached beneath the lid, feeling around with his covered hand. After a moment, he said, "I've got it."

He pulled out a long, thin glass jar. Rolled up inside was a parchment of some kind. I picked up the lantern, shining it closer to the jar to get a better look. Rutgon also stepped up beside me, staring at it in wonder.

"It's a scroll."

Bianca's voice brimmed with excitement. "Perfect. Bring it to me."

Elvis and I momentarily ignored her, lost in the historical significance of the find. The parchment looked perfectly preserved. The glass top had been sealed with a similar wax as the coffin and had no evidence of debris or tampering. Whatever the document was, I was certain it would be a national treasure of some kind.

"I said bring the jar to me. *Now.*"

Elvis blinked, and in the glow of the light, his eyes hardened. I knew in an instant, he had a plan. His eyes met mine and I gave an imperceptive nod of my head to let him know I was in, whatever he had in mind.

Without a word, Elvis turned and tossed the jar to Rutgon. They were standing close to each other, so it wasn't a big toss, but Rutgon's eyes widened in surprise at the sudden movement. He instinctively reached out, catching the jar with one hand and cradling it protectively against his stomach, nearly dropping his gun.

"That was really stupid, dude."

I thought he might shoot us right there on the spot now that he had his treasure, but the excitement of the discovery proved to be more seductive.

Rutgon shoved his gun in his waistband and held up the jar with both hands, examining it in wonder. Clearly exasperated, Bianca barked an order in Italian to him. Frowning, he lowered the jar and began to walk toward her.

That's when the screaming began.

Rutgon dropped the jar and it shattered on the stone floor. He clutched his hands to his stomach, shrieking in agony. He staggered toward Bianca. She shouted at him, but he was beyond hearing her in his pain. His guttural screams ripped at my eardrums and he fell into Bianca, clawing at her for help. I didn't even know I'd squeezed my eyes shut and covered my ears until the first gunshot. I opened my eyes as Bianca fired three more subsequent times, effectively putting Rutgon out of his pain. His screams still echoed in my head.

Furious, she turned the gun on Elvis. “What did you do to him?”

“I gave him the jar like you asked.”

“It had something on it. That’s why you covered your hand.”

“I wasn’t sure. It was a precaution.”

“What was it?”

Elvis shrugged. “A quick-acting poison, I’d guess. Acid, perhaps. It’s hard to tell.”

“It couldn’t have lasted all these years.”

“It was perfectly preserved and, as you see, it did.”

The incident had shaken her. Good, I thought. Nerves made people do stupid things. Although in this particular case, I hoped stupid didn’t involve executing the rest of us immediately. Our saving grace was that was she wasn’t sure what to do with the treasure.

“Pick it up.” She motioned at me with her gun toward the parchment that lay on the floor. “Do it.”

I dared a protest. “Look, Bianca, it’s a very old document, certainly fragile. It’s already been compromised. We might destroy it by simply touching it.”

“Don’t be stupid. If it was acid on that bottle and some of it got on the document, it will be destroyed anyway. I need to know what it says. Pick it up and read it. Now.”

Elvis brushed past me and knelt near the parchment. He used his shirt to sift through the broken glass and gently pick it up. He held it dangling from his covered hand so not to touch it. Surprisingly, it held together.

“It’s strong parchment.” Elvis peered at it.

“Read it aloud.” Bianca stepped closer. “What does it say?”

I stepped closer and held up the lantern. I could see writing, but at my angle, I couldn't make it out.

Elvis cocked his head and peered at the words. "I don't know. It's in Italian."

I could almost hear her thinking. She wanted to take a look at it herself, but she'd have to take her attention off us. Without another person to help her, that would be potentially dangerous.

She made her decision. "Bring it here. If you try anything the first one to get it will be him." She pointed the gun at Xavier. "Your twin, I presume."

Elvis paled.

To my surprise, Basia spoke up. "Wait. I speak Italian. I can probably read it."

Bianca considered and then nodded. Basia walked over to Elvis and me. She was shaking, too, and I tried to give her a brave smile.

"Don't step in the glass," Elvis warned her. "And don't touch the document."

She slid up to his side and peered over his shoulder sideways at the parchment. I tried to angle the lantern in a way that would help her.

She blew out a breath. "Okay, it's definitely in Italian, but the writing is old-fashioned. It almost looks like a recipe."

Bianca stepped closer. "What kind of recipe?"

"It's a list of chemicals. No, not chemicals. Medicinal elements. Oh, God, I'm just not sure. Let's see. There are words like opiate, morphine, phosphorus, hyoscyanus, nitric acid, and a slew of other homeopathic elements. I suppose it could be a prescription or recipe. I don't know."

Elvis frowned. "Morphine, hyoscyanus, opiates. It sounds like an anti-suppressant."

Basia gasped. "Wait. Oh, my God. Oh, my God. It's signed Leonardo da Vinci."

"*What*?" I peered closer. "Da Vinci? Where? Are you sure?"

Basia made a squealing noise in her throat. "Yes. Oh, my God. I'm not kidding. Look there. His signature. It's right in the corner. At the bottom."

Even Elvis's hand shook a bit as he squinted at the writing. He was either excited or freezing without a shirt. It was too hard to tell.

"It's possible," he said. "Melzi was the executor for Leonardo's estate. He would have had access to all of his papers after his death."

I glanced at Basia. "Then why would Melzi hide it in his mother's crypt in a glass coffin?"

Basia shook her head and continued reading. After a moment she gasped and looked up at me, stricken. "Lexi. It says *infezione soppressiva*, which means suppressive infection. There's a list of symptoms. It…it sounds a lot like AIDS."

My eyes met Elvis's in the glow of the lantern as the full implication of what we were holding hit me.

I lowered the light. "Da Vinci was working on a chemical formula to treat AIDS or something like it."

Basia blew out a breath, her eyes widening. "No, no. That's impossible. They didn't have AIDS back then."

I considered. "Maybe not in the form we know it today and certainly not in an epidemic form. But it's entirely possible to speculate they could have been dealing with isolated cases."

"They were scared the formula would be destroyed." Elvis spoke quietly and held my gaze. "Either da Vinci or Melzi or both. Just like today, I'd venture a guess there were elements of society that considered it a purposeful or inflicted illness. They must have believed that if hidden long enough, perhaps society would be more accepting or at least ready to find a cure. Thus, the intricate, not to mention, spectacular hiding place."

I turned, glanced over at Bianca. "The pharmaceutical company. Maisto. That's why they want this. They're paying you to get this. They somehow knew about the existence of this recipe. Once Slash got involved, they must have contacted you. They knew you had a connection to him and they needed inside intel on how we were progressing in terms of cracking the encryption. You weren't advising SIMSI on our progress, you were informing Maisto."

Bianca didn't answer.

"It's a risky proposition, you know." Xavier spoke up from across the room. "This so-called cure could be worth absolutely nothing."

I pressed the back of my hand to my forehead. "True, but I tend to agree with Elvis. What's the point of hiding it in a crypt and booby-trapping the jar if it didn't have some potential?"

Basia frowned. "Yeah, and what's with the killer poison?"

I lifted my shoulders. "Who knows? Probably dissuading grave robbers or the casual thief. It was common technique used in ancient Egypt to protect the pharaoh's sarcophagus and its treasures. Besides, any decent historian wouldn't touch a potentially priceless document without taking proper precautions, like gloves, anyway. I think it means the recipe must have worked, at least to some extent. Either da Vinci instructed Melzi to protect it for the future of mankind or Melzi was smart enough to figure it out for himself. I mean, come on. Da Vinci drew a freaking helicopter in

1493. It took us more than four hundred years to finally figure out how to build one. Who's to say what lurks in the mind of a genius? He might present a chemical and medicinal combination no one has thought of before."

"Chi and prana." Elvis spoke quietly. "A medicinal prescription. Alchemy, like you said, Lexi. That's what the hieroglyphics were trying to tell us."

"Jeez." The mere thought of it staggered me. "Do you guys have any idea what we have here? This could be huge. Potentially life-changing for all of mankind."

"And very lucrative for me. Wrap it in his shirt and bring it to me." Bianca pointed the gun at me.

"If I wrap it, I might destroy it."

"That's a risk I'm going to take."

Suddenly we heard a faint noise behind Bianca. Everyone froze, listening. Voices. They were faint, possibly back at the graveyard itself, but it meant we had more company. Whether the voices were attached to the good guys or the bad, it was impossible to tell.

Bianca apparently didn't know either. "Bring it now."

Elvis laid the parchment on the floor, unwound his shirt from his hand and handed it to me. I laid the material out flat and began to carefully roll the parchment in it. When I finished I stood and handed it to Elvis.

"No. You bring it to me." She pointed at me. "You're going with me. Depending on who is out there, I may need a hostage."

Elvis held out his hands. "Take me instead. It will be easier to control a smaller person. I weigh less than she does."

"Hey." Despite our dire circumstances, I felt mildly insulted.

Bianca shook her head. "Her. Now."

Exhaling a breath, I walked toward her. She took

the parchment from me, tucking it gingerly in the inside pocket of her leather jacket. Then she shoved me toward the door and pulled something small, black and circular out of the pocket on her jumpsuit, palming it and pushing a small red button. The device began to hum and tick.

I stared at her with my mouth open. "You've got to be freaking kidding. Is that a bomb?"

She tossed it and the device rolled against the lower part of the dais and stopped. Before I could move, she shoved me out of the room, slammed the door shut, pocketing the key.

"Go." She shoved the gun hard into my lower back, forcing me forward.

"Are you totally insane?" I shouted. My brain was on overdrive and I thought I might puke and faint at the same time. "No, wait. Don't answer that. Of course, you are. You're going to kill them."

"And you, too, if you don't move it. We've got ten minutes to get out of here."

She shoved the gun into my throat and I gagged and staggered sideways. At that moment I knew for certain that I was going to have to take her myself…or die trying. I decided not to think too closely about it. Geek girl taking on Italian secret agent super bitch. Yeah, calculating those odds would be fun.

I turned my back to her. As Bianca pushed me again toward the first tunnel, I had a moment of clarity. I realized that the only weapon I had readily available to me was math and it just might be my salvation. A plan began to form and I let my feet drag as my brain went into super overload. People who don't like math and think they will never use it in their ordinary lives, they couldn't be more wrong. Math was everywhere, and if my calculations were right, math might possibly save my life.

Figures raced like wildfire through my brain. The distance between the tunnel and me. The distance between my back and Bianca's gun. The velocity at which I'd have to enter the tunnel. The seconds it would take to turn my body to a right degree angle in the tunnel. The projected distance between Bianca and me the moment she entered the tunnel. So many calculations. I needed more time. Except I didn't have more time. No time for double-checking or experiments. There was a freaking bomb ticking away just steps from me and if I didn't do something, people were going to die.

Get your game on, Lexi Carmichael.

I took a deep breath. I could do this. First order of business... I needed to make her angry.

Bianca pushed me again from behind and my brain calculated how hard and far I stumbled after receiving the push. It wasn't enough. I needed her to push me harder. I figured it shouldn't be too hard to piss her off.

"You know, Bianca. I really can't believe Slash dated someone like you. You do realize you dress like a ho. Oh, sorry, maybe your English isn't good enough to understand that. Do you know what a hooker is? I mean what's up with all that spandex? Plus Slash and I were laughing about how we could tell you've had plastic surgery on your lips and boobs. All I can say is it's a good thing he dumped you so quickly."

She pushed me again, and this time, I almost fell. My brain re-calculated the velocity of the harder push and I liked it much better. Theoretically, my plan could work, but she had to give me at least one more hard push as we approached the tunnel. If I didn't resist but fell into it, the speed should be enough. *Should* being the operative word here.

Ticking bomb.

Homicidal psycho.

No pressure.

"He did *not* dump me. It was a mutual parting. Now move."

I took a step forward. "That's not what he told me. When we talked about you, he said you were ah, needy, clingy. Especially cold in bed. The worst sex experience of his, um, considerable repertoire."

"Shut up, bitch!" She slammed the gun into my kidney with a vicious push, harder than all the previous ones. This time I leaned forward with it, using the motion to dive into the tunnel, my hand already slipping into my pocket.

One, two, three. I fell hard on my left side just as my right hand pulled the perfume from my pocket, flicking off the top with my thumb. Four more seconds and she was in the tunnel with me, the gun held out in front of her, exactly as I had calculated. Without hesitation, I sprayed the perfume directly at her eyes as my right leg kicked at the gun in her hand. She screamed, but to my dismay did not lose her grip on the gun. I sprayed again and she fell backward, screaming. Dropping the bottle, I grabbed for the gun. It went off and a hot sensation ripped through my left hand, but I managed to wrench the gun from her. Bianca fell backward out of the tunnel just as I got control of the gun and fired it wildly in her direction. She screamed again. I pushed out of the tunnel just in time to see a flash of steel heading in my direction. I ducked but the knife sliced along the back of my shoulders leaving a burning trail. If hadn't been for her impaired eyesight, I would have probably been skewered like a roast pig.

For a moment, we just stood breathing hard, staring at each other. Me holding the gun. She holding the knife. Her eyes still streamed with tears from the perfume I'd sprayed and she held her side. Blood leaked between her fingers. My God, I must have hit her. My stomach heaved and my left hand was a bloody mess, but I remembered precious seconds were literally ticking away. That gave me a weird deadly calm. This was it. The moment of truth. Either do it or die. I tightened my finger on the trigger. I had no idea how many bullets were left, but I was about to find out.

I stared at her. "Drop the knife."

She didn't move so I raised the gun. I took a second to calculate distance and hold my hand steady before I shot the knife out of her hand. She screamed in shock and pain as the knife clattered to the floor.

"Now, give me the key."

She bent over clutching her hand. "You're crazy. What if I don't?"

"I'm not a geek girl for nothing. The next shot I take is a head one. You just dumped a bomb in there with my friends. I don't have a lot of time or options."

She paled and reached into her pocket. I surprised myself by how steady my finger stayed on the trigger. Life or death. Funny how that had such a sedative effect. I had maybe four or five minutes left to save my only friends in the whole world. Their lives depended on me and I would *not* fail them.

She tossed me the key and I picked it up. I knew what I had to do. Trying not to fall apart, I walked over closer.

"I'm sorry, Bianca. Really I am. I didn't want to have to do this, but sometimes life sucks."

Without hesitation, I pulled the trigger.

Chapter Sixteen

I ran to the cave door, shaking so badly, I could barely slide the key into the keyhole. Dizziness swept through me and I couldn't catch my breath. I finally heard the click and I threw myself against the door with all my weight. It opened with a grinding noise and astonished faces looked my way.

Everything else seemed to happen in slow motion. The gang knelt near a small hole in the corner of the cave and I realized they had buried the bomb to try and limit its blast. They were throwing dirt on it, patting it down. But what shocked me the most was not only was Slash alive, but he was conscious and free of his hand and leg cuffs. One side of his face was dripping blood, but he was breathing and alive. Our eyes met across the cave. He gave me a grin and I burst into tears.

Basia ran to me first, nearly knocking me over in a hug. Her shirt was missing and for an instant I fixated on the absurdity of why she wore only a purple bra. Then I snapped back to reality.

"Hurry!" I screamed and pushed her past me. "Get out of here. Get out."

Elvis straightened as well staring at me in shock as if I were an apparition. He was still naked from the waist up and now covered in dirt. "Lexi!"

"Run," I shouted and my voice sounded funny to my ears. "God, run, Elvis. Hurry."

He started running, but not toward me. "Tito is still alive." He skidded to a halt next to Tito. He was still unconscious, but it looked like someone had pressed a compress against his wound. That's when I realized it was Basia's shirt.

Slash and Xavier ran to help with Tito. The twins got Tito across Slash's shoulders and he managed to carry him out of the room on his back. Xavier pulled the door shut while Elvis and Slash got Tito into the tunnel. Elvis got in first and pulled Tito along. Slash ordered Xavier to climb in next and do what he could to help Elvis pull Tito through.

I ran over to Bianca and tried to grip her beneath her armpits and pull her to the tunnel, but my left hand would not cooperate. It hurt like crazy and I was shaking so badly, I could barely stand. Slash put a hand on my shoulder, calming me.

I threw my arms around him, sobbing into his neck, slick with blood. "You're alive. I thought you were dead."

"Get in the tunnel, *cara*. I've got her."

"I shot her." I sobbed like a maniac. "I sprayed her with Nonna's perfume and then I shot her, Slash. Three times. On purpose. She fainted or died. I don't know which."

Slash leaned into me, giving me a hard kiss. "*Mio Dio*, I'm so in love with you. She's still alive. Just get in the tunnel. That bomb will go off any second."

He bent down and propped Bianca up, getting a good grip under her arms and dragging her behind him.

He frowned when he saw me still standing there. "I said hurry, *cara*."

I stumbled toward the tunnel and crawled in as fast as I could with my injured hand. I could hear shouting and screaming ahead of me, and Slash's heavy breathing and grunting as he pulled Bianca. I felt light-headed from loss of blood or unimaginable stress. It was too hard to tell. Either way, I feared I'd pass out at any moment.

I was nearly to the end of the first tunnel when a hand stretched out to me. I grasped it with my good hand and saw Elvis's face framed in the tunnel opening as he pulled me toward him.

I was holding his hand when the bomb exploded.

I had time only to register the sound, the feel of the tunnel quaking beneath me, and a single curse word in Italian. Then nothing else but the feel of Elvis's hand against mine as darkness engulfed me.

Chapter Seventeen

I dreamt I frolicked in a meadow with yellow and pink flowers, the sun warm on my head and shoulders. Butterflies fluttered around my hands and the wind blew through my hair, lifting it from my neck and offering a cool reprieve from the heat. I laughed as a butterfly landed on my finger. I watched in delight as it fluttered its wings in a strange dance. My delight faded when after a moment, it no longer looked like a butterfly, but a weirdly shaped spider. Surprised, I tried to shake it off my hand, but it bit my finger and held on as pain spread along my hand and up my arm.

I twitched, shook, and then tried to open my eyes. My eyelids felt as if they weighed a hundred pounds each. Somehow, I got them open. I could see nothing but a giant blur. I blinked a few more times and then squeezed them shut as a wave of pain swamped me. As soon as the pain subsided, I opened my eyes again. I could see a bit better. It was dark, but there was a dim light. I tried to lift my hand where the spider had bit me, but a bandage completely covered it. An IV had been stuck in my arm and. someone had dressed me in a hospital gown. I patted the bed beneath me. I was in the hospital?

"Lexi?"

I blinked and turned my head. Elvis stood next to the bed. He took the hand that wasn't bandaged and squeezed it gently. "How do you feel?"

I opened my mouth, but nothing came out. I swallowed, my mouth dry.

"Water." It came out as little more than a croak.

Elvis picked up a pink jug and poured some water into a plastic cup. He held it to my mouth and I took several greedy sips.

I leaned back against the pillow and tried to organize my thoughts. I still felt as though I were floating. "I'm…in the hospital?"

Elvis took my hand again and it helped anchor me to reality. "Yes. Do you remember what happened?"

I tried to think back. Where had I been? Why was I in the hospital?

I frowned. "I… I can't remember."

"The cave? Bianca? The bomb? Anything ring a bell?"

The bomb. There had been a bomb…in a cave. Bianca. The woman who had shot Tito and fought with…

Memories flooded back. I gripped Elvis's hand. "Slash?"

"He's alive. He just got out of surgery. He's two doors down. Part of the tunnel collapsed on you guys when the bomb went off.

I lifted his hand. Our fingers were linked together. "You had my hand."

He nodded. "I didn't let go."

I sighed, closing my eyes. "I almost got you killed. Again."

"I don't recall you throwing a bomb in the cave."

"You wouldn't have been there…if I hadn't called you."

He leaned over and kissed my cheek. "I wouldn't have missed it for the world. You sure know how to show a guy a good time."

"What would I do without you?"

"Hopefully you won't ever have to worry about that question."

I smiled and then my eyes popped open. "Basia and Xavier? Are they okay?"

"They're fine. Shaken, of course. We all are. They're out in the waiting room, sleeping. They'll only let one of us in here at a time."

"Tito?"

"He's still in surgery."

"I still can't believe she shot him point-blank."

Elvis sighed. "I know. Bianca's dead, Lexi. She didn't make it. Slash was dragging her behind him. The tunnel collapsed completely on top of her. Both you and Slash risked your lives for her."

"I shot her." Tears filled my eyes. "Three times."

"You didn't kill her. She suffocated. You saved us from her, Lexi. Geek queen saves the day. You were magnificent. I thought..." His voice caught and he paused. "I thought I'd never see you again. Then you opened the door and you were back."

I remembered. I remembered everything.

Elvis, Xavier and Basia patting dirt on top of the bomb. Slash alive, standing up, bracing himself against the wall. Rutgon on his back in a pool of blood. Tito lying still on the dirt floor.

Tears leaked down my cheeks and Elvis brushed them away with the pads of his fingers. "Rest now, Lexi. We'll talk more later."

"Okay. Elvis, will you hold my hand until I fall asleep?"

He lifted my hand and kissed it. "I'll be around for as long as you need me."

I closed my eyes and held his hand tight. "I think that's going to be a long, long time."

There was a pause and then he whispered, "Good."

This time when I woke, my memories were intact and my hand and head hurt a lot less. I looked around, but I was alone in the room. I managed to sit up and push the sheet aside. All my limbs were intact, although my legs were black and blue, and my left hand was still hidden beneath a mitt-like bandage. I had an IV in my arm and what looked like a catheter. Jeez.

I glanced around until I found the nurse call button. I pushed it and a woman in a white shirt and slacks appeared within seconds.

"Uh, hi." I didn't know if she spoke English.

She smiled at me. "Is everything okay?"

"You speak English?"

"That's debatable. I'm from the Bronx."

"Ha. You're American?"

"Transplanted. My husband is Italian."

"Ah, that makes sense. Can I get this out?" I pointed to the catheter.

She nodded. "Sure. Lie back, please."

It took her a few minutes to take care of it and I asked if I could get out of bed. I walked slowly around the room on wobbly legs, dragging my IV around with me. It felt good to be up and moving around a bit, even if it was exhausting. After a few minutes, the nurse helped me back into bed.

"So, what exactly happened to me?" I asked her. "Am I okay?"

"You'll live. You had a gunshot wound to the hand.

The surgeon repaired some of the bone and muscle damage and sewed you up. You should have full use of your hand with just some minor scarring. You'll need an extended period of antibiotics though and some physical therapy. You also got badly banged up." She pointed to my head and legs. "You were knocked out from falling debris. You've got a black eye and a couple of serious bruises on your jaw and cheeks. Looks like you had a run-in with a truck. Not to mention the six stiches from what looks like a knife wound across your back."

I winced remembering how much it hurt when Bianca had sliced at me.

She touched the right side of my head. "You also had a concussion. Something fell on you, probably a rock. Apparently you were found in a partially collapsed cave."

"Tunnel."

"You're lucky you didn't break any other bones."

"Or suffocate."

"That, too."

I asked her to help me prop up the pillows. "How much longer do I have to be connected to the IV?"

"It's up to the doctor."

"Okay. There's a patient two doors down. A man with long dark hair. He was in the tunnel with me. How is he doing?"

"He's currently sleeping off the effects of the surgery. He is one lucky guy. He had a bullet buzz the side of his head, a severe concussion, a broken ankle, fractured elbow and a dislocated shoulder. He was in shock by the time we got him. But he's strong. He should pull through."

I let out a deep breath. "Wow. That's good he's doing okay. Really good. There was one more guy…"

"Yes, you all were brought in together. Believe me, the nurses and I are dying of curiosity to find out what happened to you guys. We've even started a pool. But we've been instructed by the police in no uncertain terms that we are not to ask."

"The police?"

"Yes, and apparently not the regular police. Special agent police. It's all so exciting and super-secret. There are police and security everywhere. Half of them are in the waiting room, pacing around like caged lions. I'm supposed to let them know when you're ready to talk. Are you?"

I thought for a moment. "Not yet. If you don't mind."

"Sure, it's no skin off my nose. Anyway, I'm sorry to say the prognosis for the other guy is still unknown. He was in bad shape when they got him here. He was in surgery for seven hours."

I closed my eyes. "Can you ask the doctor when I can remove my IV?"

"Sure. You should rest now."

"Sounds like a plan."

The next time I opened my eyes Basia stood next to an unfamiliar man in a dark blue sweater and slacks. She smoothed back the hair on my forehead and smiled at me.

"You know you're my hero, right?"

"Jeez, Basia. Don't embarrass me."

She laughed. "Lexi, this is Dr. Dioli. His English is limited so I'll translate for you."

"Okay."

She said something to the doctor and he spoke back to her. Basia turned to me.

"He said you requested your IVs to be removed and he's fine with that as long as you promise to take your antibiotics and pain killers. They checked your hand this morning."

I looked down at my bandaged hand and realized it was no longer encased in a mitt, but had only a white bandage wrapped around the middle. I could see my fingers. I tried to flex my hand, but it hurt. I winced.

"You'll start physical therapy tomorrow. You up for it?"

I exhaled a deep breath. "A hacker needs her hands, right?"

She grinned. "Right."

Dr. Dioli removed the IVs, checked my vital signs and then patted me on the shoulder and left.

Basia pulled up a chair. "How are you feeling, Lexi?"

"Glad to be alive. How are the twins?"

"Worried sick about you."

"The police?"

"They were the ones at the graveyard. They were locked onto a microchip that is apparently connected to Slash. When his vital signs went into distress, it set off the chip. The Italians were dispatched to find him. To say they were surprised the chip led them to an open crypt is an understatement. Then the bomb went off. They've been understandably busy since pulling us out of the crypt. We've been debriefed. Elvis and Xavier led them to the Vatican money in Rutgon's offshore accounts. We told them all about Rutgon and Bianca. Two people at Maisto have already been implicated and they are talking. There may be more."

"Good. How did Maisto know about da Vinci's work?"

"Apparently a private collector of some of da Vinci's personal papers came across a reference to a clue hidden in a painting called *God's Plague* painted by none other than his protégé, Francesco Melzi. The clue supposedly pointed to a secret chemical recipe da Vinci was working on to cure a friend who had a "suppressive infection." Melzi claimed to have concealed the recipe in a secret place, the location of which was revealed in the painting. The only problem, *God's Plague* wasn't publicly available. They couldn't study it to find the clue. It was hidden in the depths of the Vatican archives."

"The *secret* archives. I still don't see the connection to Maisto."

"The collector sold the information to someone at Maisto. That person, apparently in conjunction with others, felt it a worthy enough case to investigate."

"Worthy as meaning potentially worth billions of dollars worldwide if they were the sole owners of a cure or prescription to prevent or treat AIDS."

Basia nodded. "Exactly."

I sorted through the implications. "Okay, so they needed to find a hacker to attack the archives, so they brought on Rutgon. They had him cause an electronic diversion to take everyone's attention elsewhere while he penetrated the archives. The only problem is that while Rutgon was good, he wasn't good enough to hack into the Vatican Bank or the archives. That's where Serafina came in."

"Yes."

Basia rubbed her temples, looking exhausted.

"Are you okay, Basia?"

She nodded. "I'm fine. Really. Just exhausted from dealing non-stop with the officials. Not that I'm complaining about the fact that I'm alive, mind you."

"I'm with you on that."

She sighed. "Lexi, you should know there are Italian and American agents all over the hospital, not to mention a slew of priests and representatives from the Vatican. It's a freaking circus. They'll want to interview you and Slash as soon as you're able." She leaned back in her chair. "The whole thing is all over the news. Internationally. Finn has been calling every ten minutes to get a status update on you. On the up side, X-Corp is now famous. Looks like we'll have our jobs for a bit longer."

"Good thing I was discreet. Ha." I rolled my eyes and it hurt. "How are Slash and Tito?"

"Slash is alive, sexy even in a hospital gown, and asking about you. He's a terrible patient. Tito..." She looked at the floor. "They're not sure he's going to make it. He has a priest with him now, just in case."

I swallowed hard. I couldn't bear to think about it.

She patted my hand. "Look, Lexi. I'll hold off the investigators a bit longer. Take some time to process everything. I know that's important to you. Let me know when you're ready. Okay?"

I nodded. "Basia, I'm glad you're my best friend, although I don't know why you put up with me half the time."

She laughed. "You just saved me and you want to know why I adore you? You kick it, girlfriend. Always want you on my side. You know I love you. Now go to sleep. We'll all be back in the morning."

I hadn't even known it was nighttime. She stood, pulled her chair back to the corner of the room and headed for the door. I stopped her before she pulled it open.

"Wait, Basia. I've got one more question. Do you know where my clothes are?"

Chapter Eighteen

I must have dozed a bit because when I woke, I was hungry and thirsty. But first things first. I carefully sat up, swung my legs to the side of the bed and walked to the bathroom. I felt much stronger, probably because they were no longer pumping so many drugs into my system. When I came back to the bedside, I poured myself a big glass of water and drained it. I wiped my mouth with the back of my hand and then padded to the door to peek out.

After a moment, I slipped into the empty hallway, using a hand against the wall to brace myself as I walked along the corridor. Two doors later, I entered the room. I could hear the steady rhythm of breathing. There was a small light near the bed and I saw Slash, his head swathed in a bandage, his right arm and shoulder in a sling and his right leg elevated and in a cast. He was dressed in hospital garb, but I could see his gold cross gleaming in the light. I bent down and then squealed as his hand shot out, capturing my wrist.

He opened an eye. "*Cara?*"

"Slash. Jeez. Good thing we are in a hospital. You about gave me a heart attack."

He released my wrist and smiled. "You're okay."

"I'm in better shape than you."

"I'm glad."

My legs were shaky, so I half sat on the bed next to him. "How do you feel?"

"Better now that you are here."

"Rutgon shot you."

"*Si*. Thank God he wasn't a sharpshooter. Still the bullet grazed my head and the shock of it knocked me out. I must have hit my head hard on the ground, adding insult to injury. All in all, I'm lucky to be alive."

"You could have killed him earlier. Rutgon, that is. You put down your gun for me."

"I wasn't going to let him shoot you, *cara*. I'm fairly confident I could have taken out both him and Bianca, but I couldn't risk it. I couldn't risk you."

I swallowed hard. "Did you hear the police arrested some people at Maisto and they're talking, confessing to a bunch of things? Basia and the others have already been debriefed."

"I heard. I've already been debriefed myself."

"You have?"

"*Si*. I told them you had little else to add for the time being. I wanted to give you time to rest, to think things through."

Jeez. My friends knew me so well. Guess that was what friendship was all about. No matter what else we were, Slash had truly become my friend.

I looked down. "Bianca didn't make it."

He took my hand, threading his fingers with mine. "You didn't kill her, if that's what you're thinking."

"I know. Honestly, I don't feel guilty about that, well, not too much. She would have killed all of us if I hadn't stopped her. I understand that. But if it hadn't been for me shooting her, three times, she might have made it out of that cave alive. So, in a way, I'm responsible."

"Not true. She made her own choices. Bianca betrayed her country, her colleagues, her church, and herself. For money. Don't forget that. She forced you into an ugly choice."

Intellectually, I knew he was right. Emotionally, I was having a harder time with it.

"Is that what your job is about sometimes, Slash? Making ugly choices? Is that why you carry a gun and sometimes seem so sad and detached?"

He sighed. "*Si.* Sometimes. It doesn't make for an easy life. But we are born to be who we are. I'm good at what I do and I like to believe I help more people than I hurt."

I lifted his hand and saw the raw marks where the handcuffs had rubbed the skin raw. "How did you get the handcuffs off?"

"Rutgon still had the key in his pocket. Elvis retrieved it and freed us."

"Oh. Good thinking." I'd forgotten about that.

He touched my cheek. "How did you disarm Bianca?"

"By sheer luck. I sprayed her with Nonna's perfume once we got into the tunnel, then we fought for the gun. While we were struggling, it went off and got me in the hand before I could get control of it. Then I shot her in the side, mostly by accident. She had a knife and wouldn't give me the key. There was no time to argue, so I shot the knife out of her hand. After that I popped her in the knee so she couldn't follow me to the cave and stop me from helping you guys. It was weird, Slash. Like I was another person, calm and completely detached from my body. I just kept shooting. Boom, boom, boom. What happened to me? Am I a monster?"

Slash took my hand and pressed it to his cheek. "It

makes you incredibly brave, *cara*. You did what you had to do for survival. We both know you could have killed her with one shot and ended it there. But you didn't. Instead, you tried to save her despite the fact she would have murdered all of us. That makes you smart and very, very human."

I felt better hearing his words. "I'm sorry, Slash, but I lost Nonna's perfume. I dropped it in the tunnel. I hope she didn't want it back. It was undoubtedly the best present I've ever been given, in spite of the questionable smell."

He chuckled and then winced. "There you go again. Making me happy."

"You're not just saying that to sleep with me, right?"

"*What*?"

"Never mind. Do you know anything more on Tito?"

Slash frowned, then sighed. "No. Apparently it's touch and go. I've been praying."

I envied him his faith. There was something to be said for having a bastion of hope to draw upon. How cool that he truly believed in divine intervention and the well of hope that accompanied it. Well, if anyone deserved divine intervention, it was Tito. I sincerely hoped Slash's prayers worked.

"So, I guess this means Uncle Benedetto is off the hook."

"It does. The Vatican is very pleased with X-Corp's efforts."

"And yours. Unofficially, of course."

"Of course." He squeezed my hand. "Basia told me about the da Vinci parchment and how you and Elvis retrieved it from the coffin."

"We're a good team."

"We all are."

He let out a breath. "Basia said da Vinci might have been working on a prescription to treat an AIDS-like virus. It's too bad we lost it after all this time, not to mention the glass coffin and the historical significance either items might have held. The authorities said no documents were found on Bianca's body."

"Well, that's because I relieved her of the parchment after I shot her in the kneecap. We may have lost the coffin, Slash, but we've got the prescription. I tucked it in the inner pocket of my windbreaker. I'm afraid to unroll it from Elvis's shirt in case I ruin it, and I don't know how well it fared the bombing, but at least I've got it. I checked earlier tonight and it's still in my coat."

Slash looked at me, incredulous. "I… I don't know what to say, *cara*. You are simply extraordinary."

"Well, I'm being taught by the best, right? You said it yourself. You're the teacher and I'm the pupil, right?"

He smiled and crooked his finger at me. "Come closer, pupil. There's another lesson I'd like to teach you."

I leaned down and he slid his hand behind my neck, pulling me to his mouth. He kissed me gently, his lips still hot and sexy even though he lay in a hospital bed.

"I was born when she kissed me," he murmured against my mouth.

I lifted my head. "Humphrey Bogart. Again."

He smiled. "*Si*, from his movie *In a Lonely Place*. Bogart was a man who knew what he wanted. I admire that."

He pulled me down for another kiss.

My head spun when he finally released me. "Are you sure this is a good idea, Slash?"

"Trust me, *cara*, it's the best medicine in the world."

"I do. Trust you, that is."

He smiled and I slid my feet up on the bed and curled up next to him. He tucked a blanket over me and we talked about things that didn't involve bombs, guns or death until we both fell asleep.

Chapter Nineteen

"I'm not sure this is a good idea."

I'm positive I'd said that about four hundred times, but no one was listening to me.

Basia fussed with a ribbon on my dress. "This bow is not lying flat."

"I don't like bows. Can't we just take off the belt?"

Basia pursed her lips. "Don't make me hurt you."

She apparently fixed the bow to her satisfaction because she let go of me and smiled. "Perfect."

I looked like a dork. It had been a week since we'd been pulled out of the crypt and I still didn't feel quite like myself. I'd been released from the hospital and the twins, Basia and I were staying in the *Hotel Atlante Star* while the Roman police, the Italian secret service, Vatican officials, scientists from the National Roman Museum, and members of the American Embassy took our statements. I'd turned over the Da Vinci Recipe, as we had started calling it, to the Roman authorities. We were told that the parchment was still readable with minimal damage. Scientists, historians and medical researchers were beyond ecstatic at the find. How the medical implications would play out, no one knew yet, but everyone agreed it was a priceless historical find. In the meantime, I continued to be debriefed and questioned on every aspect of what had happened, so much so that I began to dream about it. In Italian.

At some point we were informed that the Pope had invited us to a private meeting so he could thank us personally for assisting the Vatican. I hadn't thought it a particularly good idea given my sucky social skills and lack of etiquette knowledge, but I guess in Italy one didn't say no to the pope. As none of us had proper attire to wear to such a meeting, Finn offered to foot the bill and we had all been forced (except Basia, who went screaming with happiness) to go shopping.

I wished I could have clothes shopped with the twins, but they went off to a guy store and Basia dragged me to a girly boutique. There had been a lot of discussion with the saleswoman about Italian fashion, sparing no expense, and leather shoes. It had been nothing more than a blur to me and I had spent most of it sitting in a chair watching, but Basia had been in fashion heaven. She bought herself a dark green dress with matching pumps and a purse to match. She talked me into buying a knee-length royal blue dress with a soft belt that tied into a loose bow in the back and a pair of shoes to go with it.

I'd put on the outfit in the hotel and Basia had adjusted it and brushed my hair like a million times, leaving it long and loose. She put some cream on my hair and fluffed it, saying it shone like rich sable. I wanted to pull it back in a ponytail, but she wouldn't let me.

After that came the makeup to hide my fading bruises and make me look a little less scary. Basia put creams and powders all over my face and eyes. When all was said and done, I thought she'd managed to do a pretty decent job of disguising the purple and black marks without it looking too over the top.

"Stop fussing." Basia frowned at me. "Go talk to someone. Smile a little. It's an honor to be here. Stop being anti-social."

I glared at her. "I'm *not* being anti-social. I'm just not being user friendly."

She rolled her eyes and I sighed. She was right. It was an honor to be here. Besides, I was glad to escape the relentless interrogations of the authorities even if it meant engaging in social niceties. I think Basia was glad, too. In spite of her annoyance with me, she looked excited and happy—totally in her element. Diamond studs sparkled in her earlobes and her dress swished prettily every time she moved. She made looking feminine seem so effortless.

It all felt terribly awkward and I was beyond nervous about meeting the pope. We'd already had a meeting with the monsignor in charge of protocol. He explained the dress code, social expectations, requirements for genuflection, and the list of topics I was and was not permitted to talk with him about. After he was done, I couldn't remember a single thing I was supposed to do. My brain had shut down after I heard the words papal audience. Besides, I had already decided to nod at everything and not open my mouth. Not even once.

Now, as we waited outside the door, I fidgeted and stood close to Elvis. The twins looked amazing in matching dark blue Italian suits, red ties and loafers. Thankfully they looked as nervous as me.

Elvis put a hand on my shoulder and whispered in my ear. "You look pretty."

"You're just saying that to make me feel better. I don't feel very feminine with a bandage on my hand and make up that barely hides my hideous bruises."

"No, I mean it. You really do look nice. Your hair

looks shiny and soft." His face turned a slight shade of red.

I touched my hair. "You're right. It does feel soft. Want to touch it?"

He cleared his throat. "Okay. Sure." He ran his hand down the length of my hair twice. "It is soft, and it smells nice, too."

I sniffed at it, wondering what Basia had put on it. "Well, you guys look beyond amazing. Handsome and distinguished. Have I ever seen you in a suit before?"

"No."

"It's a good look on you."

"Thanks."

I shifted my weight on my feet. My new shoes were uncomfortable. "So, are you up for hobnobbing with the pope?"

He shrugged. "Not really. Meeting famous people is not my thing. Just between you and me, I'd rather be involved in a serious session of omphaloskepsis."

I laughed as Basia came up behind me and put a hand on my shoulder. "I heard that. Are you guys talking geek again?"

I grinned. "Not really. Elvis just told me he'd rather be at home contemplating his navel."

"*What?*"

"Omphaloskepsis. Navel-gazing."

"That is *so* not a word."

"That *so* is."

She shook her head. "Seriously. You people are so totally weird sometimes."

I laughed again, feeling much better. Being with Elvis always relaxed me. I decided to stick close to him, letting him lead the way on social etiquette. It was sort of like the blind leading the blind. But we are who we are, so I decided to go with it.

Suddenly the door opened and a priest stepped out. “Please come in.” He invited us into a small reception hall.

Basia smiled, practically pushing the twins and me inside. My nervousness increased. I felt like throwing up and hoped the whole thing would be over in minutes. Surely the pope was a busy guy. He’d smile, we’d smile, he’d thank us, Basia would say something appropriate and we could all go home. I hoped.

There was no pope in evidence yet, but a small group of priests chatted in a corner of the room, looking relaxed. I guess they had a lot of experience at this kind of thing. We stood around, pretending to mingle, until Basia gasped. I turned to see a priest coming through the doorway pushing a wheelchair. Tito, dressed in his colorful Swiss Guard dress uniform and still connected to an IV drip, gave us a smile and a thumbs-up.

We all rushed him at once, hugging, patting him on the back and talking so fast he couldn’t answer a single question. He laughed and held up his hands. I felt tears prick my eyes and saw that Basia was crying as well.

He looked over at me. “Hey, Lexi, I hear you saved the day, yah?”

“Not alone. It was *so* a group effort. You included.”

“You’re going to have to give me the full version someday.”

“That’s a deal and I’ll throw in a couple of plates of gnocchi to go with the story. How are you feeling?”

“I’ll survive. I’ve got some rehabilitation ahead of me, but I should make a full recovery.”

“I’m glad to hear that. I’m even happier because I really *really* wanted to see you in those pantaloons.”

He smiled. "I told you hope was a godly pursuit. So, here I am. I'll tell you a secret. They actually look better when I'm standing up."

"They look pretty good when you're sitting down, too. By the way, I promise not to touch your shirt anymore."

"Yah? I meant to tell you I usually I have dinner with a girl before I let her pull off my shirt."

I blushed.

"Dude." Elvis gave him a high five and slapped him lightly on the shoulder. "I can't tell you how good it is to see you."

Tito grinned. "It's going to take a lot more than one of Nico's old girlfriends to bring me down, yah?"

"She wasn't my girlfriend."

We turned around again. Slash stood in the doorway, leaning on crutches. He was dressed in a navy three-piece Italian suit with a sky blue tie. The right side of his head was partially shaved and still bandaged on one side, but he looked shockingly handsome. His right leg was in a thick cast up to his knee, but his sling had been removed. Beside him stood Nonna, dressed to the hilt in a fancy white blouse and flowered skirt. Her white hair had been done up in a bun and she even wore make-up. I sniffed the air and smelled her strong perfume as she marched right up to me. At first I thought she was going to hit me, but instead she threw her arms around me. She kissed me on both cheeks and gave me a hug benefitting a linebacker. Then she burst into tears.

"Oh, jeez," I said, squashed against her tiny frame.

She pulled away and smashed my cheeks between her palms. She said a bunch of words in Italian and then kissed me again. I'm pretty sure I'd turned at least six shades of pink by the time she was through.

Basia stepped up beside us. "She thanks you for saving Slash's life. For saving all of us. For honoring Italy."

I was at a loss for words. "Ah, tell her the perfume saved us. It was the most fortuitous gift I've ever received. Oh, and tell her I work for food. Her food to be exact."

Basia translated. Nonna smiled through her tears and then held my hands. She said something else. Basia giggled and then coughed. Then giggled again.

I glanced at Basia. "What? What did she say?"

"She said you're welcome to have Slash's baby."

"*What?*"

Basia lowered her voice. "Is there something you haven't told me?"

I glanced over my shoulder where the priests stood. "Jeez, Basia. Do we have to discuss this right now?"

She patted Nonna on the shoulder and said something to her. The older woman returned to Slash's side just as Uncle Benedetto and a middle-aged couple were escorted through the door.

I recognized the couple. "Hey, those are Serafina's parents. I saw their picture on her desk."

Basia nodded. "Slash made sure they received an invitation. He called them personally and told them what happened to Serafina."

"That was nice of him."

Benedetto waved at me and I waved back. Before he could approach me, one of the priests came over and hushed us. The pope was about to make an entrance.

My nervousness returned and I sidled up to Elvis. I linked arms with him and held on. Like me, Elvis had a photographic memory. I just hope that *unlike* me, he'd been listening to the monsignor when he explained everything we were supposed to do in the presence of the pope. I'd do what he'd do and hopefully not make too much a fool of myself.

The pope entered the room and I was struck by how normal he looked. Intellectually I knew he was just a man, but his persona was so larger-than-life that it seemed odd that he seemed so…regular.

Everyone in the room starting applauding quietly. Elvis clapped, so I clapped, too. The pope spoke a few words to in accented English, thanking us for what we had done, recovering the stolen Vatican funds and returning the digital file of the painting stolen from the secret archives. Then the pope walked over to where Tito sat in the wheelchair. Tito bent his head and the pope said a few quiet words to him before offering Tito his ring. Tito kissed the ring and the pope squeezed his hand and made the sign of the cross over him.

Elvis leaned close to my ear and whispered. "The ring is blessed. For Catholics, kissing it indicates a sign of respect and affection."

"Do I have to kiss it, too?" I whispered back.

"No one *has* to kiss it. But most Catholics do."

"I'm not Catholic."

"Okay. You can shake his hand then. Weren't you listening to the monsignor?"

"Isn't the answer to that already obvious?"

Elvis rolled his eyes. "Just remember to genuflect, Catholic or not. Follow my cue."

"Got it."

The pope approached Slash next. Nonna immediately genuflected but as Slash was on crutches, he was only able to dip his head. To my astonishment, and apparently the others in the room by their collective gasp, the pope hugged him. Then the pontiff spoke in a low voice with his hand resting on Slash's shoulder for at least a full minute before offering his ring. Slash kissed it and the pope made the sign of the cross over both him and Nonna.

I held my breath as the pope straightened and searched the crowd. After a moment, his eyes fell on me. I held my breath and squeezed Elvis's arm so tightly he grimaced. When the Pope got closer, Elvis bent to one knee. I realized he was genuflecting so I followed suit.

The Pope stood directly in front of me. "Lexi Carmichael?"

I liked the way he said my name. It sounded nice with his soft Spanish accent. But there was no way I was opening my mouth and sticking my foot in, so I just nodded.

"It seems the Vatican owes you a big debt."

I shook my head.

"We greatly appreciate your efforts on behalf of the Catholic church and the Holy Order, including risking your life to bring an end to the treachery and deceit of others. Good deeds do not go unnoticed."

I smiled brightly.

After a long pause, Elvis nudged me in the side with his elbow. Oh, jeez. I think that meant I had to say something. I was probably defying protocol or causing a major affront by not speaking.

I genuflected again, just in case. "Um, it was no problem, Your Excellency..."

Elvis coughed. "Holy Father."

"...Holy Father. It was my sincere pleasure." I stopped, considered my words and to whom I was speaking. "Well, truthfully, and I know it's important to you that I am truthful, it wasn't a pleasure because the situation itself wasn't pleasurable. No, there's nothing pleasurable about shooting people. So, I'd like to make it clear that I did not, in any way, find pleasure in shooting anyone. Thou shall not kill. I got the memo on that one. Did you know I've actually read the Ten Commandments and other parts of the Bible, too?"

Oh, jeez, I was babbling. I *knew* I shouldn't have said anything. The pope probably thought I was a complete moron. "Anyway, I'm glad I could help out. So…we're good, right?"

I winced and glanced over at Slash. He'd closed his eyes. Somehow, I didn't take this as a good sign.

The pope held out his hand to me and smiled. "We're good."

Relieved, I shook his hand. Vigorously. When he let go, I saw he'd pressed a small silver crucifix into my palm. When I looked up, he made the sign of the cross over me and moved on to talk to the others in the room. After he'd met and spoke with everyone individually, he thanked us all for coming and was escorted out by the monsignor.

I breathed an enormous sigh of relief at his departure and turned to Elvis. "Oh, jeez, tell me the truth. How awful was I?"

"You were magnificent."

"Really?"

"Really. Your comments were genuine and heartfelt."

"You're just saying that."

"Pretty much."

I opened my hand and examined the crucifix. "Did he give you one?"

Elvis shook his head.

"I wonder why he gave it to me?"

"That's a no-brainer. You're special."

I glanced up. "I am?"

"You are. And I'm not just saying that. It's true."

I smiled. "Thanks, Elvis."

"Sure, anytime."

I took a minute to chat with Uncle Benedetto, who gave me a bear hug and kissed me on both cheeks just as Nonna did. He told me I was now a part of the family and to come visit him in Italy anytime. I also spoke to Serafina's parents, telling them what a smart daughter they had and how sad I was for their loss.

Eventually I made my way over to Slash. He chatted with everyone in the room, but sometimes I felt his eyes on me. When I looked over, he smiled a funny smile at me.

I waited until no one else was with him and walked over to where he sat, his crutches propped up against the chair next to him. I sat down in an empty chair.

Before he could speak I held up a hand. "I know, I know. You don't have to tell me I made a fool of myself in front of the pope."

"Ah, contraire, *cara*. He will always remember you."

"Yeah, as the doofus who babbled about not killing people."

"No. As the woman who saved the Vatican eighteen million euros."

"Well, there is that."

"*Si*, there's that, indeed."

I opened my palm. "He gave me this."

Slash took the crucifix from the palm of my hand. "He knows," he murmured.

"He knows what?"

"That you're special."

"That's odd. Elvis just said the exact same thing."

Slash's gaze fell upon Elvis, who was chatting with Tito. He sighed. "He knows, too."

Slash put the crucifix back in my palm and closed

my fingers over it. But he didn't take his hand away, just left it there holding mine.

I studied the bandage on his head. "So, how are you feeling?"

"Tired. Exhilarated. Ready to get this cast off my leg."

"Oh, a man of many moods…not to mention many names." I shifted in my chair. "You do realize we almost died and I still don't know your real name. Aren't you ever going to tell me?"

He regarded me thoughtfully and then released my hand, crooking his finger. "Come here, *cara.*"

I leaned toward him.

"Closer."

I slid to the edge of my chair, nearly lying on top of him. He pushed the hair back from my shoulder, put his mouth up to my ear and whispered something.

I pulled back, searching his expression for a hint of mischief. "No freaking way."

"Way."

I narrowed my eyes. "You wouldn't lie to me in a house of God, would you?"

"I wouldn't lie to you *ever.*"

I sat back in my chair, studied his face, and tapped my foot. "It totally fits. I can't believe I didn't guess it."

"No?"

"No. Jeez."

Slash watched me in amusement.

I lifted my hands. "Well, there it is. Just like that. Thrown down like a gauntlet between us. I can't believe I finally know your real name. Can I call you that, you know, in front of other people? Or shall it remain secret for all of eternity?"

Slash grinned. "I'll make you a deal, *cara.* As long

as you promise to call me, you can use whatever name you want. You won't have to worry. I'll come to you."

I grinned back at him, glad to be alive, glad to be his friend or whatever it was we were.

He stuck out a hand so we could shake on it. I took it and his fingers curled warm and strong around mine.

"So, do we have a deal?" he asked.

I shook his hand. "We have a deal. That's one promise I'm sure I can keep... Romeo."

* * * * *

Read on for an excerpt from No Biz Like Showbiz, *the next book in the Lexi Carmichael Mystery series from Julie Moffett.*

Acknowledgments

A book is rarely a singular effort and *No Place Like Rome* is no exception. Carina Press editor Alissa Davis provided numerous suggestions that made this novel a much stronger one. Other than myself, there is probably no one who knows Lexi better! Thanks are also due to my parents, who count themselves among Lexi's biggest fans. They were willing volunteers (well, guinea pigs) to do the first beta read and they offered much-needed encouragement and advice. But most of all, I'd like to acknowledge you, the readers, who have bought my books and took the time to send me an e-mail or write a review about the adventures of Lexi and the gang. You are the fuel to my muse. From the bottom of my heart, I thank you. oxo

About the Author

Julie Moffett is a bestselling author and writes in the genres of mystery, young adult, historical romance and paranormal romance. She has won numerous awards, including the Mystery & Mayhem Award for Best YA/New Adult Mystery, the prestigious HOLT Award for Best Novel with Romantic Elements, a HOLT Merit Award for Best Novel by a Virginia Author (twice!), the Award of Excellence, a PRISM Award for Best Romantic Time-Travel AND Best of the Best Paranormal Books, the EPIC Award for Best Action/Adventure Novel. She has also garnered additional nominations for the Bookseller's Best Award, Daphne du Maurier Award and the Gayle Wilson Award of Excellence.

Julie is a military brat (Air Force) and has traveled extensively. Her more exciting exploits include attending high school in Okinawa, Japan; backpacking around Europe and Scandinavia for several months; a year-long college graduate study in Warsaw, Poland; and a wonderful trip to Scotland and Ireland where she fell in love with castles, kilts and brogues.

Julie has a B.A. in Political Science and Russian Language from Colorado College, an M.A. in International Affairs from The George Washington University in Washington, DC, and an M.Ed from Liberty University. She has worked as a proposal writer, journalist, teacher, librarian and researcher. Julie speaks Russian and Polish and has two sons.

Visit Julie's website at juliemoffett.com.

Watch the Lexi Carmichael series book trailer at Youtube.com/watch?v=memhgojYeXM.

Join Julie's Facebook Reader Group at Facebook.com/groups/vanessa88.

Follow Julie on Social Media:

Facebook: Facebook.com/JulieMoffettAuthor

Twitter: Twitter.com/JMoffettAuthor

Instagram: Instagram.com/julie_moffett

Pinterest: Pinterest.ca/JMoffettAuthor

My name is Lexi Carmichael and I have a problem with most of today's television programming. Not because of the sheer implausibility of a majority of the shows—although that does factor—but because too many programs seem to feature a tech genius who can solve the problems of the world with one stroke of a keyboard.

Here's how it happens…a tech head is desperately trying to hack into a system. Death, the collapse of the free world, or the apocalypse is imminent if he fails. (Yes, tech heroes *always* seem to be guys, since I guess in Hollywood a woman doesn't know her way around a keyboard.) *He* types commands frantically as the clock ticks down to doomsday. As the scenario continues, our frazzled hero takes a moment to run his fingers through his perfectly styled hair before he types just one more command and bingo, he's in. He'll then have a whole millisecond to navigate a completely unfamiliar system, find the magic switch, and shut down the entire system in time to save the day, world, girl, whatever, with one stroke. All of this while the super-expensive, cutting-edge government system or expensive black-market technology used by the show's villain will aid our intrepid hero by providing helpful visual prompts like Access Denied or Access Granted in big bold letters across the screen as he works his hacking magic.

Just shoot me.

I'm a *real* hacker and yes, I'm female. I double-majored in mathematics and computer science at Georgetown University and have spent most of my twenty-five years learning how to bypass cryptographic protocols, exploit system vulnerabilities, and finesse distributed denial of service attacks. I've never had to avert an apocalypse, but if I did, I'm pretty sure it would take more than one freaking minute, and I wouldn't be worried about my hair while doing it. My first successful hack on a relatively simple system took five hours. It might have taken four, but my mom kept distracting me by yelling through my bedroom door that if I gave ballet class just one more try she'd give me a hundred dollars to spend however I wanted. So, watching these types of shows and movies is hard on both my nerves and stomach.

Despite this, I still have a television and occasionally go to the movies. Although I never did learn to dance ballet, I did create a place of solitude for myself in a small apartment in Jessup, Maryland, which is near the National Security Agency, where I used to work. Now I'm the Director of Information Security for a hot new cyber intelligence firm in the DC area called X-Corp. The job title sounds impressive, but I'm still the same girl I've always been, except I've been trying hard for the past several months to expand my social horizons outside my safe virtual cocoon. That means I'll watch television once in a while just so I can have something to talk about if the conversation lags, which it inevitably does if I'm involved.

On Mondays, I generally eat dinner in front of my laptop while gaming and watching *Repercussions*, a sci-fi cable series about a group of young adults who discover they're the prodigies of a race of super aliens. However, I'd seen this episode, "The Savant Within," so I'd muted it to concentrate on my game.

My game is "Hollow Realm," an online real-time strategy scenario where players command magical armies in massive and complicated battles against each other. My best buddies, Elvis and Xavier Zimmerman, genius twins and excellent strategists at "Realm," were remotely supporting my current struggle against a bunch of demon-controlled ogres. It wasn't going well.

I ate another spoonful of my dinner—Cheerios—and tried a couple of virtual maneuvers with my army of Glimmers—shimmery forms that could use light to destroy an enemy. Mistake. A group of frenzied ogres with light-deflecting shadow shields called murks crushed me.

"Crap. Total failure."

Dejected, I pushed my chair back from my monitor. I'd have to try to recoup my losses another day.

My computer pinged me. I glanced down at the message.

Better luck next time, Lexi.

I typed back.

Thanks, Elvis. You and Xavier rock. Appreciate the support. Let me know if you need help with the zombies on Zeroth.

Will do. Hoping for pizza and Quake with you soon. How are you feeling?

I'm good. Going back to work tomorrow. I look forward to that pizza and more gaming soon. Miss seeing you.

Me too. A lot. Bye.

Bye.

I stared at the message for a moment. Just a few years ago I never would have imagined one of my best friends would be a guy, let alone one of the few people in the universe who could beat me at most online fantasy role-playing games. But now, Elvis probably knows me better than anyone. We're mirror images—two awkward geek rulers within the world's new cyber-universe, while we remain outsiders in the real world. It's a nice feeling to know he always has my back in both worlds.

I drank the rest of the milk from my bowl and carried it out of the bedroom. I'd taken one step into the kitchen when I saw a man dressed in jeans, a dark sweater and a short black leather jacket leaning against my counter.

"*Slash!*"

I jumped a good foot straight up and lost control of my bowl. Slash caught it and the spoon with one hand.

"Easy there, *cara.*" He put the bowl in the sink, then turned to face me.

Slash is one of the most fascinating and complex people I've ever met. He's Italian-American and probably the sexiest überhacker in the universe. He works for the National Security Agency in some top-secret capacity, and his knowledge is so important and integrated with the security of the United States that a team of FBI agents follows him around the clock.

Slash and I had just returned from what had turned out to be a dangerous case in Rome. Typically, hunting hackers doesn't involve bodily harm, but this case had been an unusual one and we'd both nearly died. I'd been shot in the left hand and was still rocking a line of stitches across my back.

He grinned. "How are you doing?"

His black hair was shorter on the side of his head that had been injured and he also had a walking cast on one leg. All of that only served to make him look even sexier and more mysterious than usual.

I pressed my hand to my chest. "Well, not counting the five years you just took off my life by showing up unannounced in my kitchen, okay, I guess."

It's kind of a running joke between Slash and me. No matter what kind of alarm I buy or how I set it, he gets into my apartment. I don't think he's ever once knocked on my door. It used to freak me out, but now it's just part of our game.

"How about you, Slash? You feeling any better?"

He carefully rotated his shoulder. "The doctor took the sling off two days ago. It's feeling pretty good. I've got some physical therapy ahead of me to get it back to full strength."

"That's great."

He took a step across the kitchen and gave me a kiss on the cheek. He smelled good. He *always* smelled good. "I've been thinking about you, *cara*."

He took my left hand in his and turned my palm up. "You got the bandage off. How does it feel?"

I flexed my hand. "It hurts, but it's better. I'm so used to the twinges I barely notice it. I have to squeeze a therapy ball thirty minutes a day. I'm going back to work tomorrow." I glanced down at his leg. "How's the cast?"

He leaned over and tapped his leg. A hollow thump

sounded. "It's uncomfortable. I must wear it for another two weeks."

I sighed. "Jeez. We're a couple of wrecks."

"*Si.*" He put his arm around me. "But it's better than the alternative."

"True. Well, since you're here, do you want to sit down?"

He smiled and I led him to the couch. As he sat down, I saw a shoulder holster and gun peek out from beneath his jacket. I helped him prop the leg with the cast on the coffee table before sitting next to him and leaning back against the cushions. I put my feet on the table next to his.

Slash is another anomaly in my life. I'd met him when we both got mixed up in an international case while we working at the NSA. At some point, over the past few months, our relationship had evolved. It happened so subtly I couldn't put my finger on when or how exactly it occurred. But something had definitely changed between us in Rome, so now I had to calculate what it meant in terms of everyday interaction with him.

"Slash, there's something I've been meaning to ask you."

"Ask away."

"We're friends, right?"

"Absolutely."

"Is that all?"

He shifted slightly on the couch, studying my face. "What's on your mind, *cara?*"

"Well, back in the crypt in Rome, you said…you said you loved me."

My cheeks heated. Why was I embarrassed? I wasn't the one who had said it. Slash had uttered those three words, throwing them down like some kind of gauntlet between us. Unfortunately, we'd been running from an armed bomb at the time, so I couldn't ask for clarification. Now that we were home, was I supposed to do something—say something—in response? If so, what?

"Ah, *si*, I did say that."

Holy cow. Slash *loved* me. My stomach felt funny and fluttery at the same time. "So, did you say that for a reason, or was it a turn-of-phrase-because-we-are-in-serious-peril kind of thing? You know, in case we bought the farm."

"Bought the farm?"

"Died."

He chuckled. "No. I said it because I meant it. I *am* in love with you. Quite desperately, actually."

I searched his face for signs that he was teasing. But he met my eyes with a calm, even gaze. "Define what you mean by love."

He touched my hair. "Italians do not define love. We show it. It became clear to me in Rome—actually, *you* became clear to me. I realized that you had become the most important thing in my life."

"I had? How?"

He sighed. "Where to begin? I think you've surprised me in ways I never expected. In addition to your intelligence, you are one of the most genuine, open and courageous people I've ever met. There is no pretense with you. No hidden agenda in the relationship."

"Why would anyone have a hidden agenda?"

"Why, indeed?" He fell silent.

I hesitated and then plunged on. "Well, I feel it's important to point out that you've omitted any mention of my lack of social graces."

He shrugged. "They are overrated. I haven't always got it figured out either."

I blinked. "You haven't?"

He chuckled. "I haven't. *Cara*, I've faced my share of social bullying, even as an adult."

Slash, bullied? The man who seemed to handle people and complex situations with effortless grace? The same man who attracted women like electrons attracted protons?

"You, Slash? That's…impossible."

"Why? I was overweight and oversmart when I was young, and kids can be quite cruel."

"I'm sorry. I understand the trauma of bullying quite well. But you seem so confident now."

"At some point, I lost the baby fat and eventually figured how to use my intelligence to my advantage in social situations. But I was still more comfortable with computers than with most people, even girls."

"Wait. *You* had problems with girls, too? Really?"

He laughed. "*Il mio Dio*, I adore you even more. *Si*, really."

I held up my hand. "Well, at least you've had relationships. I can count the number of friends I have on one hand, and I've never been in an, um, romantic relationship with anyone on a boyfriend-girlfriend level."

He took my hand. "Good."

"Why is that good?"

"Because I like the idea of being your first significant other."

"You want to be my significant other?"

He raised an eyebrow. "Would you like me to be?"

I considered his words. "I… I don't know. What about Finn?"

Slash sighed, dropped my hand, then crossed his arms against his chest. "What about him?"

Finn Shaughnessy is my boss and a guy who still wants to have a talk with me about a relationship that we may or may not be having. I'm having mixed feelings about Finn. I'm physically attracted to him, but I've been slowly coming the conclusion that I am not going to be able to date him—if that's even what he wants—mostly because I don't think I can handle the complexity of dating my boss.

"I'm not certain of my relationship status with him."

Slash's voice hardened. "Finn is not my concern. How *you* feel is what matters to me."

"Fair enough. But how do you sort it all out? How do you ascertain you've accumulated enough information to decide whether or not you're going to enter into a romantic relationship with someone?"

"When you want to be *with* someone, you'll know."

I'd know? Who was he kidding? I never knew about stuff like that. *Never.*

"We're talking beyond just the physical attraction, right, Slash?"

"*Si*, that's right."

I paused, thinking about what it would be like to have sex with Slash. Okay, I'll admit I'd thought about it before, but now his declaration of love had really put it on the table. No question I was attracted to him and, based on the number of intimate touches and kisses he'd given me in the past, it seemed clear I appealed to him. I still couldn't fathom why. A guy as hot and accomplished as Slash could easily have his pick of any woman on Earth. So, why he liked me remained a bit of mystery. For me, the easy part was my attraction to him—both physically and intellectually. The hard part was the emotional attraction and how to define or even sustain that so that it equaled love or at the very least, an intimate relationship on more levels than just the physical.

"It just doesn't seem logical to rely on what might be the heat of the moment or an intangible concept like love to enter into something as important as a relationship."

Slash's jaw tightened. "You'll figure out what you want from Finn. I cannot do that for you. All the same, I want you to know I'm here and I'm not holding back any more. You opened the door to me in Rome and I stepped through. I'm not going to back off, Finn or any other man notwithstanding. But you should know, if I enter the game, I play to win, especially if the reward is something particularly valuable to me."

This statement seemed significant. I remembered something my best friend Basia had told me once about Slash being a player. She said guys like him enjoyed the thrill of the chase, but lost interest after the win.

"Is love a game to you?"

Slash linked fingers with me again. "I admit that it has been for me in the past. But with you, no." He pressed his lips to my palm. "Never. Believe me, if it was just a game, I would have had you in my bed long ago."

I didn't want to ask, but I knew I'd regret it if I didn't. "So, is that the end game? You know, sex?"

He looked surprised at the question and then chuckled. "Sex is not the end, *cara*. It can be the *beginning* of an intimate connection. But in our situation, there are so many aspects that are completely out of my control. Sex isn't going to resolve those. Only you can, when you're ready."

"Wait. We have a *situation?*"

"I'm afraid we do."

I studied him. "You're actually worried. What could you possibly be worried about?"

"*Tu mi hai rapito il cuore.*"

"What did you say?"

"I said you have stolen my heart."

"I did?"

He pressed my palm against his chest. "*Si*, you have. As a result, the power of this relationship belongs to you. Perhaps it has from the first moment I saw you in your bedroom in that ridiculous T-shirt, boldly testing my hacking skills. Then, when you kissed me in Rome, I knew for certain."

"How?"

He shook his head. "I don't know. I just did. Because of that, I'm not going to make you, trick you, or even seduce you into choosing me, as much as I'm tempted. And you should know I'm tempted very much. I want you to come to me willingly, with an open heart, because then it *will* matter. Not only to me, but to you and your heart."

My pulse quickened. "Define willingly."

He laughed and kissed the top of my head. "See, that is exactly why my heart is yours. I'll define nothing more. You'll know when you know. Just inform me, at some point, if you consider Finn, or anyone else, your boyfriend so I can figure out how to manage that. Deal?"

"You could manage that?"

"I could. Just promise me you'll keep me informed."

He made it sound easy, like I could figure things out just like that. But he was Slash and things like that always seemed to come easy for him, despite what he'd said about his past.

I sighed and put my head on his shoulder. "Okay, I promise."

Don't miss No Biz Like Showbiz *by Julie Moffett, available now.*
www.CarinaPress.com